Praise for Pam Mantovani...

Of *Cowboy on Her Doorstep* . . .

A great romance story, full of emotion and real-life characters who steal your heart from the first page.

—*bestselling author Rita Herron*

"If you love second chance books this is for you. I cannot wait for the next book from Pam Mantovani. Keep them coming Pam!!"

—*Goodreads reviewer, Melissa Morr*

Of *Cowboy on Her Porch* . . .

"It's been a while since I've read such a good book. Once I started, I couldn't stop reading. The author did a great job developing a relationship between Carter and Audra, and did not rush "the relationship like many authors tend to do."

—*Goodreads reviewer, Amy Vida*

Of *The Christmas Baby Bargain* . . .

"This is by far my favorite Christmas romance. Filled with hope, love, miracles and a sweet, cuddly baby this book will become your favorite too. Pam writes with an understanding of the relationship between a man and a woman and then adds just enough conflict, tension and magic to help them become a family. You can't help but fall in love with them too. It's one I will read again and again."

—*Amazon reviewer, M. Lee Scott*

Of *Cowboy to Her Rescue* . . .

"Cowboy to Her Rescue by Pam Mantovani is a heartfelt, passionate and truly moving story that I'm sure many romance readers will find hard to put down."

—*Amazon reviewer, Arch_Angel*

"The storyline is deeply emotional, and the character portrayals are unpretentious and likeable. This is an easy-to-read story that I finished within a couple of hours due to the ebb and flow of the writing and the engaging and meaningful relationship between Sydney and Ryland."

—*Goodreads reviewer Karen Roma*

Books by Pam Mantovani

Cowboy on Her Doorstep

Cowboy on Her Porch

The Christmas Baby Bargain

Cowboy to the Rescue

Cowboy Under the Mistletoe

Cowboy Under the Mistletoe

by

Pam Mantovani

Bell Bridge Books

This is a work of fiction. Names, characters, places and incidents are either the products of the author's imagination or are used fictitiously. Any resemblance to actual persons (living or dead), events or locations is entirely coincidental.

Bell Bridge Books
PO BOX 300921
Memphis, TN 38130
Print ISBN: 978-1-61026-170-8

Bell Bridge Books is an Imprint of BelleBooks, Inc.

Copyright © 2021 by Pam Mantovani

Published in the United States of America.

We at BelleBooks enjoy hearing from readers.
Visit our websites
BelleBooks.com
BellBridgeBooks.com
ImaJinnBooks.com

10 9 8 7 6 5 4 3 2 1

Cover design: Debra Dixon
Interior design: Hank Smith
Photo/Art credits:
Package/Bow (manipulated) © Illustrart | Dreamstime.com
Couple (Manipulated) © Chernetskaya | Dreamstime.com

:Lucm:01:

Dedication

To Deb

for the magic of a long-ago red pen

for a single red stitch on a quilt

for the continuity of a treasured friendship

Chapter One

SINCE COMING TO Burton Springs, Montana, as the town interim doctor, as well as tending the surrounding hundred-mile countryside, Dr. Gabriella Santini had treated a nasty bite on the shoulder from a skittish horse, injuries to hands and feet from combine blades, hay bailers, and tractors, and a sprained foot when someone was stepped on by a cow who objected to being shoved into the branding chute. All were a far cry from what she'd be doing at home—the gunshot or knife wounds, the scramble to prevent death due to a drug overdose or alcohol poisoning, or using her surgical skills for any number of reasons during her residency in her hometown of Chicago.

Today she would be dealing with a hand wound from a rooster attack.

This wasn't the first time she'd driven to Evergreen Ranch, the ranch designed to serve as a retreat for military personnel to reacquaint themselves with their families, following deployment. Six weeks earlier, on a beautiful late September afternoon, the grounds had taken on a fairytale feel as two people she considered friends exchanged vows. While her romantic Italian heart was happy for Ryland and Sydney, the day had been bittersweet for Gabriella. It had been a reminder that a betrayed relationship was the reason she was currently in Montana.

She'd needed time, and distance, to heal her heart. And her pride. And it had worked. The only drawback was that she missed her close-knit family.

"Two months left," she murmured, a little surprised at the realization, as she drove beneath the overhead iron sign announcing her arrival at the ranch. Her mother had promised the family would postpone their Christmas celebration until Gabriella returned home at the first of the year.

Parking in front of the cookhouse, she grabbed her medical bag and stepped out of the SUV. Sidestepping the inch of snow on the ground, she headed inside. "Ellen?" she called out.

The ranch cook came through the swinging doors that led to the kitchen, wiping her hands on a bib apron. "You made good time in the snow."

Gabriella smiled. She wondered just how long she'd have to live here before people believed she knew how to handle the weather. Any argument she'd made about living in Chicago was usually met with a tolerant smile. After all, everyone knew there was more snow in Montana. She unwrapped the scarf she'd knotted at her throat and unbuttoned her coat. "The roads are clear. So where's the patient?"

"In Sydney's office." Ellen waited for Gabriella to hang up her coat before she led the way. "It should be interesting to see if she's let go of Van yet."

"Van?" Gabriella asked. She'd crossed paths with the tall blacksmith several times, and had admired the delicate iron gazebo he'd built for Ryland and Sydney's wedding. "What's he doing here?"

"Sydney had some foundation business in Billings. She convinced Ryland to go along."

"Bet that was an easy task."

Ellen chuckled. "Anyway, Van came along with Judson to give the horses some exercise. He was the first one to reach the little girl when she started screaming." Ellen paused in front of the closed door and rolled her eyes. "From what I gather, he scooped her up into his arms and she hasn't let go of him since. Wouldn't even leave him when her father and mother came."

Gabriella walked through the door Ellen opened. In a chair, in front of the small desk, Van sat, his strongly muscled arms cradling a sniffling little girl. Standing behind him, hovering, were her parents.

"Well, hell," Gabriella said to Ellen in a low whisper. "Who could blame her?"

She used her free hand to shove her long dark curls behind her as she approached and squatted in front of the chair. "Hello.

I'm Doctor Santini."

The little girl curled a little more into Van's chest. Gabriella looked up, becoming uncommonly distracted for a minute as she stared into the green eyes that studied her. She thought he looked more frightened than the child he held. And yet he made no move to hand her over to Gabriella. Was there anything sexier than a big, attractive man protecting someone small and hurt? Not to her mind. This scene reminded her of the times in her past when her papa had protected her from life's problems. Anything to do with the love and support of family would always be irresistible to her.

"I bet you were scared when that rooster attacked you," she said to the girl.

"I just wanted to pet him."

"I never had a when I was a little girl. Do you have one at home?" Continuing to ask questions and make comments, she was able to distract the girl while she unwound the temporary wrapping and examined the wound. "You look pretty comfortable sitting on Van's lap," she said as she cleaned the small cut and applied antibiotic ointment. She flicked up a glance, smiled at the man in question.

"He scared the chickens away. But he's not mean, even though he's really big."

Gabriella chuckled, her heart softening at the faint blush that rose on Van's cheeks. "If I was hurt, I'd want him to hold me." Because those green eyes of his fired with heat, and her toes curled in her boots in response, she forced her attention back on the little girl. "There, all better now," she said once she had the hand wrapped in a bandage. *"Sei una ragazza coraggiosa."*

"You talk funny."

"It's Italian. It means you're a brave girl. My papa would always tell me that when I hurt myself and my mama had to treat me."

"Is your mama a doctor?"

"She is, a surgeon. I hope to be as good as her someday."

"You must be really smart."

Gabriella looked up and winked at Van. "Smart enough to

leave roosters alone." When the girl giggled, Gabriella leaned forward to press a kiss to the center of the bandaged palm. It wasn't something she could get away with in a Chicago emergency room, but here, it felt natural.

Rising, she looked to the parents. "It's not a deep gash."

"Thank you so much for coming so quickly. We weren't sure there would be anyone close by who was qualified to help."

It wasn't the first time Gabriella had heard a similar sentiment while in Montana, something she'd found herself contemplating from time to time. With a few whispered words she couldn't overhear, Van finally succeeded in separating from the girl and, with a nod for the parents, started to leave the room. But he stopped when the girl ran after him and tugged his hand. When he leaned down, she kissed his cheek. He looked stunned for an instant, then he abruptly left. Gabriella hurried through the simple instructions for the parents, a prescription for antibiotics, and her contact information should they have any concerns, as she repacked her bag.

Outside, after storing her medical bag in her SUV, she walked to the corral. Van was leading a horse out. "Thank you for your help," she said.

"She didn't give me much choice. I nearly had a heart attack when she screamed. Then she wouldn't turn loose of me. Even when her parents came running."

He kept a gentle hold of the reins, the way a true cowboy would. And he now wore a cowboy hat that obscured the beauty of his pale green eyes. His strong arms were covered in a thick denim jacket but she had no trouble recalling the solid strength of his muscles. Tucked inside his leather gloves, she knew his hands were wide palmed with several cuts and scars on the knuckles and back of the hand, imprints of the dangerous aspect of his job. And yet he'd handled that little girl with such gentleness.

"You were very sweet with her."

Gabriella lifted a hand, paused with a look in his direction. At his nod, she stroked the horse's forehead.

"You should have gloves on."

"I'm always forgetting them. I never had the chance to tell you how much I admire the workmanship on the gazebo you made for Sydney and Ryland's wedding. It was stunning, and really made the setting perfect for a wedding. The intertwined vines looked so delicate, but when I tried to rattle it, it held firm."

"You shook my gazebo?"

She ran a soothing hand over the horse when he flicked up his head, as if insulted on Van's behalf. "Rude of me, I know, but I couldn't resist. Where did you study?"

"I picked it up along the way."

"You're self-taught? That's amazing. I'm always in awe of anyone who has the talent to create. My papa owns a restaurant and claims some of his best recipes are the result of trial and error." She tilted her head. "I'd love to see your shop, sometime."

"There's not much to see. It's just a workshop."

"I promise not to get in your way."

"Really?"

"Just tell me where you want me. To stand," she added, delighted by the interest she saw in his gaze.

"Maybe later. Right now, I need to go. I promised Judson I'd take this one for a hard ride."

"Hmm. You rescue little girls, you're a talented artist and have a successful business, and you're comfortable around horses. You're a man of many talents, Van."

"I'm just helping out a friend."

She took several steps back, admiring the fluid way he swung into the saddle. "I'll see you around."

He touched the brim of his hat with a finger before he turned the horse. *"Mio Dio,"* she exclaimed with breathless appreciation. It wasn't the first time she'd seen a cowboy in action since she'd come to Montana. But Gabriella found her attention lingering on Van, what she could see of his butt specifically, as he rode away.

While she'd come to appreciate Montana—the scenery, the people—nothing had excited her the way watching Van did now.

Wasn't that an interesting surprise?

VAN FELT AN ITCH between his shoulder blades and knew Gabriella Santini was watching him. He didn't turn to look at her. He didn't need to. Somehow, she'd imprinted herself in his mind.

They had mutual friends, so their paths had crossed before. Nearly every time he saw her, his mouth went dry.

She had big brown eyes that sparkled whenever she smiled. He wondered if they grew brighter or darker when her passions were aroused. Her tumble of dark curls made his fingers itch. At Ryland and Sydney's wedding, she'd worn those curls pinned up so her neck had been exposed—and this time his mouth had watered. She had a lush body that filled out the dresses she favored over jeans.

He figured Gabriella's admiration of his skills would vanish in the blink of an eye if he admitted that he'd learned to be a blacksmith while in jail. It wouldn't matter that he'd chosen that sentence rather than return to the house where his father regularly beat his mother. Where he and his younger sister could never do anything right. The only reason Van had stayed there as long as he had was to keep an eye on his sister.

Until the night his father had taken one too many swings at his mother. That night, Van had unleashed years of hurt and impotence, and while he'd gotten in his share of punches, his father, who'd had a lot of experience in inflicting pain, had managed to knock him out. When Van woke, he found his hands restrained in cuffs and his mother accusing him of being high on drugs and attacking his father for no good reason.

So, at sixteen, he'd started doing time. And when he'd walked out from behind those bars nineteen months later, he'd taken off. For years he'd crossed the country, finally stumbling upon an older man who took him in, adding to his training, giving him a place to stay and the means by which to build his tool inventory. Then he'd met a woman. And he'd made the mistake of giving in to her pleas to protect her from an abusive ex. Until the night that ex had jumped him when he returned to his small room. Then he, and the woman Van had thought loved him, robbed him of every penny he owned, along with most of his tools, and left town.

He had no intention of risking everything again because he had an itch for a woman totally wrong for him. Giving the horse his head, he let the speed and the sting of newly falling snow clear his mind. Too bad it didn't work.

Driving back home a few hours after returning the horse to Judson's ranch, his mood didn't improve any when he found Mayor Marcia Scott on the workshop porch, running her fingers over horseshoes stacked to resemble a Christmas tree. "Damn it," he swore, shutting off the engine. "Why can't people leave me the hell alone." Unsure if he meant the mayor or the lingering image of Gabriella stroking her hand over the horse, he got out of his truck.

"Doing some early decorating?" she asked when he walked toward her.

"Website order."

"Shipping is going to add on a pretty penny."

"I factored that into the price." He managed a smile. "That way, they think they got the shipping free."

She laughed. With her silver hair and soft brown eyes behind her rimless glasses, the mayor looked like everyone's favorite aunt. As well as looking after the town, she also ran a successful family business, The Market, a grocery store that spotlighted locally grown produce in season and fresh meat from nearby ranches. She was thorough in everything she did, and while she appeared to be unassuming, he knew she could be relentless when focused on a goal. Which was why he felt twitchy about her appearance at his workshop.

"I don't want to be rude, but was there something you needed, Mayor? I'm behind on my work today."

"We both know you don't mind being rude when it suits your purposes. I heard you were spending the morning helping over at Evergreen while Sydney and Ryland are out of town."

He didn't bother to sigh or shake his head. This was another thing about the mayor—she always knew what everyone in town was doing.

"That kind of community spirit is exactly why I'm here. As you know, the Saturday after Thanksgiving is when we light the Christmas tree in the center of town. We'd like you to make a special topper."

"As you've pointed out, my work leans on the heavy side—too heavy for the top of a tree."

"You forget I've seen your other work. I know you can do something fine and delicate when you want." She waved a hand, dismissing his objections before he could voice them. "I'll leave the design up to you. Just make sure it's ready by that Saturday."

Taking for granted he'd agree, she passed him and headed for her car. With the door open, she paused and sent him a smile that looked just shy of wicked. "Oh, and Donovan," she said, the only person in town who used his full name rather than the shortened version he preferred. "I'll have someone from the committee check in with you in a week or so."

"Committee?"

"We want to make sure you have everything you need. Thanks, Donovan."

"Like you gave me any say in the matter," he grumbled before forgetting about the project and heading into his workshop. "And I don't need anyone looking over my shoulder."

ON LEGS THAT had garnered her considerable attention—some she wanted and some she didn't—while dancing the chorus line in Las Vegas, Rhonda Johnston hurried down the sidewalk of downtown Burton Springs—a far cry from the lights and hustle of the casinos in Vegas. Even though the sun was high in the big sky, she shivered. After more than five years in Montana, her blood still yearned for the sizzling heat of Nevada.

"Talk about sizzling," she murmured, her pink painted lips curving in an invitational smile as the sheriff's car pulled into a parking space. "Oh, yeah." She sighed with appreciation, and with the memory of just how the lean body now exiting the vehicle had felt on hers less than two hours earlier.

"Thought you were staying home this morning?" Sheriff Blake Owens asked.

She liked that he'd kept his hat off so she could see all that thick, brown hair. Recalled how it felt when she'd sunk her hands into it while he'd sunk into her. She also knew, without looking around, that people were watching them. Some with amusement, others with disdain that an elected official had chosen to live in sin with her. She'd never worried about others people's opinion of her or her lifestyle, and she didn't intend to start now. Thank God, Blake felt the same way.

"Didn't see much point." Always ready to give those critical onlookers something else to sniff about, she trailed a fingertip, painted to match her lips, down the center of his chest. She absolutely adored the way his cheeks took on a lighter shade. "You want to arrest me, Sheriff?" She leaned in, smiling when his gaze cut to the side to see who might be watching. "Put me in handcuffs?"

"No way." His lips curved. "You'd enjoy that too much."

She threw back her head and laughed out loud. Her amusement vanished, while everything inside her warmed, as he took her hands. "God, I love you, Rhonda."

"Now I'm going to arrest you," she said. "For making me go all soft inside on a city street."

"Hold that thought for later." He winked. "For now, why don't I give you a ride? To wherever you're going," he added when she again laughed out loud.

"Thanks, but I'm heading inside." She nodded behind her at the door to Tammy's Diner. "The mayor asked me to meet her."

"God only knows what she's got in mind now." He took one long look at her. "See you later."

"Oh, yeah," she breathed when he returned to his vehicle. Maybe she hadn't, and probably never would, acclimate to winters here, but it sure was a plus to have such a hot body to curl up with on those cold nights. "You can bet on that, Sheriff." With a turn reminiscent of being on stage, she entered the blessed warmth of the diner.

Keeping her coat on, she headed for a back booth.

"I swear, the two of you can damn near melt the ice on the sidewalk," Tammy said as she filled the cup in front of where Rhonda joined the mayor.

Rhonda simply smiled.

"Now," she said once they were alone. "What was so important that I had to come right away?"

The mayor stirred two packets of sugar into her coffee. "Doctor Leonard isn't coming back to town," she said, naming the long-time, lone doctor in the area. Eight months earlier, he'd lost his wife of forty-plus years. Three weeks later, he'd left town for what he'd termed a 'sabbatical'. The mayor had had to reach out to her never-ending list of contacts, and had finally managed to secure the services of Gabriella Santini for six months. Only now, six months wouldn't be enough.

"Well, hell, you told me you were afraid that would happen once he left."

"Yes, but now I've got an idea."

"About convincing him to return?"

"No. We need someone else." Using her cup, the mayor turned toward the big picture window, gesturing at the woman walking on the other side of the street. "That's who I'm thinking about. She's one half of my plan."

Rhonda shivered, watching Doctor Gabriella Santini walk down the street. She kept her coat unbuttoned over a navy dress that complimented the golden skin tone of her Italian heritage, even in this cold. Then again, she *was* from Chicago.

"Isn't Gabriella planning to leave at the end of the year?"

"She is . . . unless we can convince her to stay."

Since Rhonda genuinely enjoyed Gabriella's company, she was intrigued. She looked back at the mayor. "What do you have in mind?"

"Not a what. A who."

Rhonda shoved her coffee aside and leaned forward. "This sounds interesting."

Chapter Two

SINCE SHE HAD no scheduled appointments that morning, Gabriella decided to drive out to visit a teenage patient recovering from his first round of chemotherapy. She could have called and checked in, but one advantage to being a country doctor was the chance to have face-to-face visits, where she could get a truer sense of the patient's mindset. Once she was back in Chicago, she'd have little time for this kind of personal interaction. And if she followed her mother and grandfather into surgery, she'd have even less time to spend with patients beyond consultations prior to surgery, or follow-ups afterward.

Since today also netted her a batch of early Christmas cookies, the visit had been doubly productive.

With still hours before her afternoon appointments, and since she was in the area, she decided to run by Van's place and offer him a share of her bonus cookies in exchange for a look at his workshop. She wasn't above bribery when the situation called for it.

As she drove, she had to admit, it really was lovely countryside. While she'd missed the early bloom of spring, she'd enjoyed the short heat of summer, savored the brilliant crispness of fall. And now, with holiday season fast approaching, the cold and snow of winter looked and felt just right. She smiled, spotting cattle and horses in the fields she passed. This was so different from the busy sidewalks and high rise buildings of Chicago. And *very* different from the insulated world of a hospital.

She wished she'd taken more notice of Van when she'd first arrived. But, because her contract with the city was only for six months, she hadn't been looking for anything beyond friendship.

And though she was re-thinking that attitude now, she questioned if she was making the best decision at this time in her life. After all, what would be the point? Sure, she might indeed indulge in a casual affair, but what she really wanted was something lasting. She wanted the kind of family affection she'd known every day of her life. Wasn't that the main reason she'd been so devastated to learn of Timothy's betrayal? Because she'd convinced herself that they'd wanted the same things out of life—a love that would grow and expand when they had children, mutual friendships, shared interests and respect for their individual careers.

Only she'd been wrong. Very wrong.

Maybe Van wanted the same thing—a family—and that's why, knowing she would be leaving soon, he'd made no effort to get to know her better. Still, it was a shame . . . .

She reached over to lower the heater as she recalled that scorching look she'd seen in his eyes when they'd looked at one another over the head of a little girl. Thanks to her Italian heritage, flirting was natural to her, so she knew he hadn't been thinking of her as a friend at that moment. It gave her ego a giant boost to know she could still snag a man's attention. Especially a man as strong and masculine as Van Ferguson.

She took the turn onto a gravel road identified by a hanging horseshoe sign. Maybe, for their individual reasons, they would decide to remain just friends. But then, maybe they'd agree to enjoy what pleasure they could from one another for however long they had. She'd be more than happy with that.

Yes, she eventually wanted someone to be in her life forever. But until that time, no matter what choices they made, Van offered her the chance to have some company during the holidays, to not be alone. But was being with Van, even for so short a time, the right thing to do?

Timothy had wanted her, and he'd pursued her with a vengeance. In the end, they'd become lovers. But Gabriella had gone into that relationship believing she and Timothy would be starting a life together. This was totally different. If anything did develop between her and Van, she would expect no commitments from him beyond a temporary exclusivity. It would be a holiday fling—no more, no less.

Besides, he could always say no.

But she really hoped he didn't.

His workshop dwarfed the house in size and in height. She wondered if there was a specific reason for that difference, then decided there had to be. He didn't strike her as the kind of man to do something without a purpose. Both buildings had a wide front porch and a tin roof, and the house had a finely wrought iron inlay in the door. She was charmed by the flower boxes, covered in snow now, spaced along the walk connecting the two buildings. The doors to the workshop were barn style, shoved open in defiance of the cold day. When she stepped out of the car, Gabriella understood why. The furnace blast of heat could be felt ten feet away.

There was a display of crafted items on the porch, some were decorative in nature while others looked to have been made for a particular task. Some looked deadly. She stepped wide of them and approached the doorway. It took a second for her eyes to adjust to the interior light. But when they did, she was treated to a feast.

She hadn't come for a show, but she was female enough to enjoy the one in front of her. She had a moment's guilt over not alerting him of her presence, but it faded into fascination.

Van was bent over something, giving her an eyeful of the firm, very fine butt she'd ogled before. Then, he rose up slightly, lifted an arm and slammed down a hammer. Even through the material of his shirt, she could see the ripple of muscle in his shoulders and arm, could all but feel the vibration of power. She had studied those muscles and the bones beneath; how they worked, how they could be repaired if torn or damaged. She could name individual ones. But never before had muscles held her attention the way they did now as she watched Van move.

He stretched out the arm not holding the hammer, and placed whatever item he'd been pounding into a large pail. Steam from dunking the heated iron in water rose into the room, making her think of steamy showers.

As a woman, she appreciated a man with an inherent strength enhanced by his profession. She'd seen his tenderness as he'd held that little girl in Sydney's office, and now she saw the power that was such an integral part of his profession. She instinctively knew he'd be a considerate and yet demanding lover.

She sighed. It had been so long since she'd wanted that kind of physical closeness, since she'd felt bold enough to risk opening herself to that kind of intimacy. She felt as if something deeply buried inside of her was scrambling to the surface.

"Van."

Though she'd only whispered, had barely gotten his name past the shocking throbbing in her throat, he spun around. For a second, he looked like a warrior preparing for war. He stood with his legs apart, his wide shoulders blocking some of the early winter light shining down from what she now saw were skylight windows. His hair was more than a little damp, his jaw looked like he'd skipped a shave this morning, and his leather apron covered him from chest to knees.

The sizzle in his gaze was as strong and fierce as the heat in the room. The moment seemed to freeze, in contrast to the fire swirling between them. He was nothing like the men who'd appealed to her in the past. Then again, maybe that was a good thing.

"And you said there wasn't much to see," she said, recovering first.

"What are you doing here?"

"In the neighborhood?" she suggested with a smile, lifting the container of cookies. "I went to see a patient and his mother gave me some cookies." She scanned the length of him, noticing the signs of a hard morning of labor. "You look like you could use a break."

"I'm behind on my orders."

"You won't be able to complete your work if you don't keep your energy up. Or if you get dehydrated."

He lifted a brow. "Is that your professional opinion?"

"I'd hope someone who works in this kind of environment would have the common sense to take care of themselves."

His answer was to cross over to a workbench, lift a gallon jug and chug down about a third of the remaining water. Replacing the jug on the bench, he looked at her. "I've been on my own for a long time, Doc. Since I was a kid. I know what I need."

"On your own? What about your family?"

It wasn't heat that flashed in his gaze now. It was cold, a bitter, stinging freeze intended to stop any inquiry or, worse, sympathy.

She walked over to him. "Will you accept an offering from a friend? As long as—" she added, drawing her arm back a little when he reached for the offered container. "You share."

His grin flashed quick and sharp. Her body jerked as if an electric buzz shot through her system, hard enough that he reached out and grabbed her hand. She wasn't surprised to learn his fingers and palm were rough in texture. And yet, he held her with infinite gentleness.

"Be careful," he said. As if he'd read her mind, he took a step back. "There're things in here that can hurt you."

"I use needles and scalpels in my work. I can handle whatever you've got."

"You sound very sure of yourself."

"A surgeon can't afford not to be confident." She popped the top off the container, then took a cookie before handing him the rest. "I'm sure you understand that." Nibbling, she turned and walked around the room, well aware that he was watching her. "It takes confidence, almost as much as skill and strength, to bend iron to your will."

It was hard to believe he'd been on his own for so long. Her heart went out to him. She didn't know what she'd have done if she hadn't had her family behind her, every step of the way. And even now, she missed them, so very much. Still, she believed she'd made the right decision by coming to Burton Springs by herself, even if just for a short time. She'd learned a lot about herself in the last six months.

Van had obviously learned a lot, too, in the time he'd been alone. Otherwise, how would he have survived?

By building, she decided as she walked around the shop,

touching nothing but looking at everything. Whatever had caused the breach in his family, he'd obviously found a way to make the best of the situation.

She pointed toward an ornate belt buckle. "I admit, I always thought a blacksmith made mostly practical items."

"A belt buckle is practical—even if it is pretty fancy."

She laughed, loving these small snatches of humor whenever he relaxed. "Got me there."

"These are also popular and easy to make," he said, lifting a simple hook. "Sydney suggested I offer the option of classes for people staying at Evergreen to come over and make one."

"That's a great idea."

"We haven't come up with a plan yet." He set down the hook. "The wedding plans kind of took up her time." He glanced around the room. "And I've been busy finishing up Christmas orders."

"Use me as a test subject," she said as he set aside the cookie container, and brushed crumbs from his hands. "I'm a great student. I've been one most of my life. Teach me how to make one, no, two would be better. As a Christmas gift for my papa. He could use them to hang utensils in the kitchen. And they'll be small enough to pack in my suitcase when I go back to Chicago."

She rubbed fingertips at her temple, confused why she suddenly felt a little panicked instead of excited at the thought of returning home.

"Change your mind?"

"What? No." She touched his arm, and a sizzle of sexual awareness flowed through her fingers. It had been seven long months since she'd felt this level of attraction for someone, and now she just had to convince herself, and him, that a sexy fling was just the way to celebrate the holidays. Her pulse pounded as her mind filled with steamy images.

"This could be fun," she said, her voice suddenly husky.

"Fun? If that's the way you think, you can't work here. There's too great a chance of you getting hurt."

"I know how to pay attention. I know how to work hard when work demands it. And I know how to enjoy life when I have the chance. I'm Italian. I laugh when I'm happy, cry when I'm sad, yell when I'm angry." She jabbed a finger into his belly. It was as hard as the iron he worked with. She watched his eyes lower to her mouth, then rise back to mesh with hers. A slow liquid current of warmth ran through her.

"It's Christmas. What better time of the year to have some fun?" She waved a hand around as she crossed the room to where he'd stored interlocking horseshoes, welded together to resemble a reindeer, complete with a red nose made of an iron ball. "See? You do know what I mean. Oh," she exclaimed and stepped over to the Christmas tree, made with painted green horseshoes, a brightly colored ornament hanging inside each one. With a fingertip she traced the outline of a candy cane.

"Is it for sale?" She looked at him. "It would be perfect for a corner table in the reception area of the clinic. I decided against a real tree out of respect for patients with allergies."

"This one's already sold." Her shoulders slumped with disappointment. "But I can make you another one. It's just some simple welding."

"Then it should be simple to show me how it's done."

"Are you always this stubborn?"

"I'm Italian," she reminded him, spreading her hands wide. "C'mon, Van. Let's have some fun together."

A SHORT TIME later, after they made plans to get together in two days, Van stood in the shop doorway, watching Gabriella drive away. Her scent lingered, rising above the odor of heat and iron. He recalled her smile at spotting the horseshoe tree.

He was a man accustomed to heat, to fire. But what had blazed through him while she'd been here, what continued to burn inside him now, even after she left, was brighter, hotter than anything he'd ever coaxed out of his forge.

Having her around had been fun, but he had to be careful. He understood the damage that could happen when he lost focus and got too close to a fire.

For the last eight years, he hadn't allowed personal connections to interfere with his work or his privacy. Sure, he had needs that he'd had to take care of, from time to time. But he'd made certain the woman he was with understood that one night was all she'd have with him. It was all he could give anyone.

Doctor Gabriella Santini wasn't a one-night woman.

That made her obvious flirtation all the more confusing.

And yet, he'd agreed to work with her, to have her in his workshop. "For fun," he said, shaking his head as he recalled her plea. Fun wasn't the word that came to mind when he thought of her. Looked at her.

Fun had rarely been part of his life—before coming to Burton Springs or since. Before, he'd kept anything that made him happy tucked deep inside him. He'd learned at an early age that his father was a mean enough bastard to use any method necessary to spoil whatever Van liked. And he'd learned that lesson well. Since coming here, he'd focused on building the business, doing whatever he could to avoid attention.

What was it about Gabriella that tempted him to throw caution out the door? It was more than her looks, although there was no discounting them. She used her hands when she talked, often touching whoever she talked with as naturally as if they'd known one another for years. She was the kind of woman made to have a big family. And he had as much chance of having a family as he did of earning a college degree. On the other hand, who was he to question why the woman was interested in him?

If he and Gabriella got to know each other better, and decided to eventually act on the sizzling chemistry between them, there'd be no messy consequences or expectations for a future, no awkward silences or hurt feelings when they parted ways, no need for any of their mutual friends to take sides or toss out blame.

She'd be leaving town before that any of that happened.

ONE OF THE greatest perks of being a small-town doctor, to Gabriella's way of thinking, was the luxury of having time to spend with a patient. Especially when that patient was a four-month-old. One she'd delivered.

"He's so beautiful." Cradling the infant clad only in a diaper,

Gabriella lowered her face to tiny Beckett Montgomery's neck and breathed in the powdered innocence. Moments ago, he'd been screaming against the indignity of being stripped and examined.

"He doesn't do anything."

Gabriella grinned at her friend, Audra Montgomery, before turning her attention to Audra's eldest son, Blake, age four, who sat on the floor crashing cars and trucks with his younger brother, Bradley, who was just one month shy of turning two.

"Before long, he'll be following after you, wanting to do everything you do." She laughed softly, so as not to wake the sleeping baby. "I was the same way with my brothers."

Blake studied her a moment, his serious eyes so like his father Carter's. "I'll always be bigger."

"Yes, and that means you have to take care of him." She flicked a glance at Bradley, unconcerned about the conversation. "Of both of your brothers."

"You can start," Audra suggested, "by being a good example and putting all your cars back in the bag." When she got the expected groans, she merely lifted a brow. "The sooner the toys are picked up, the sooner we can stop by Tammy's for some hot chocolate."

"Nice use of a well-placed bribe, Mom," Gabriella said, as the two younger boys scrambled to see who could scoop up the most cars. She settled the baby on the padded bench and began dressing him again.

"Unless Beckett gets sick, this will be the last time you exam him." At Audra's comment Gabriella stilled, looked up. "He's not due for a check-up until after the first of the year, right? You'll be back in Chicago by then?"

"That's right." Gabriella turned back to the baby.

"You're still planning to come to our house for Thanksgiving next week?"

"I appreciate the invitation." With a last snuggle, she secured the baby in the carrier. "What can I bring?"

"Would you mind some sort of appetizer? That way the men will stay out of my and Ellen's way in the kitchen." She grinned. "Kendall handles clean up as we cook," she said, speaking of her sister-in-law. "And what about Christmas?" Audra asked while slipping into her coat. "Do you want to join us Christmas Day as well?"

"I'm getting a rifle," Blake piped up.

"No, you're not."

"Uh huh, I asked Santa for one in my letter."

"I want truck," Bradley said as his mother secured his knitted cap over his brown hair.

"Maybe," Gabriella said, flicking a fingertip down Blake's nose. "You know, Santa has to be careful. Maybe he'll bring you a toy rifle this year, to make sure you know how to look after a real one."

"Good save," Audra said under her breath. "Hold hands," she told her boys as they all headed out of the exam room.

"How many will be at Thanksgiving?"

"Kendall, Logan and their kids. Ryland and Sydney. Ellen. Rhonda and the sheriff, unless he gets a call. Van."

"Van?"

"Yes, I finally convinced him to join us last year. Wait . . ." Audra called to her running boys, before hurrying after them.

Gabriella stood on the clinic porch, arms wrapped around her waist as she watched Audra manage to get all the boys into her truck. The snow that had fallen last night coated the trees but it had been plowed from the streets and sidewalks. Gabriella stood a moment longer, watching a few business owners decorating their storefront windows for the holidays before stepping back into the clinic. Leaning against the closed door, she took a moment to let the silence wash over her. The pace here was so different from the rush, demands, and stress of a hospital. And yet, the work she did here, she'd come to realize, was every bit as vital.

If not for her need to get away from the everyday reminders of Timothy's betrayal, she'd be working emergency room shifts while waiting to hear whether or not she'd been accepted for a fellowship in her chosen field of pediatric surgery.

But she was here now. And she intended to enjoy the time

she had left in Burton Springs. Along with the possibility of indulging in a holiday romance.

She blushed, thinking of where that romance might lead. Being intimate with a man based only on physical appeal wasn't something she'd ever done before. She'd only ever given her body as a way to express her love and hope for the future. After all, she wanted a family, wanted a partner who respected and cherished her. Someone to love and be loved by.

But she didn't need to have that now. And this time, with Van, if she could persuade him to let loose a little, her heart wouldn't be at risk.

With the clinic quiet, and no emergency demanding her attention—she grinned at the memory of the little girl who'd been pecked by a chicken she wanted to pet—she cleaned up the exam room, then downloaded patient notes from her tablet to the main server. Exchanging her lab coat for her winter one, making sure she had her charged phone in a pocket, she stepped outside and drew in a deep breath of air cold enough to freeze her tonsils.

She made her way down the sidewalk, taking in the sight of city workers alternating banners and wreaths hanging from streetlights. In the center of town, other workers were setting up booths and the fire pit that would not only provide warmth but a gathering spot for making s'mores. A corded off section waited for the tree that would be lit on the Saturday following Thanksgiving. She snapped a few photos, and sent them to her mother in a text. Even with the pang of homesickness, she loved the festive mood in town. Inspired, she stepped into Buds and Blossoms.

"Good morning," Mary Harris, the owner called out. "It's a glorious day isn't it?"

"It is," Gabriella agreed.

In no time at all, she'd ordered wreaths for the front windows of the clinic and another for the outside entrance to the upstairs apartment. While she'd have the horseshoe tree for the clinic, Gabriella wanted something more traditional for her living space. Armed with the information that the tree lot at the high school, with proceeds earmarked for new band uniforms, would be open next week, she turned to leave . . . but paused when she spotted a trio of potted dwarf spruce trees decorated with red bows.

Well aware she was fabricating an excuse to see him, she had the three trees loaded into her car, and got in. It was time to put her 'Tempt Van plan' into high gear.

Chapter Three

"DAMN IT."

Disgusted with the lack of concentration that had him making the same mistake three times now, Van tossed the heated iron into a bucket of water. At this rate, it would be Christmas next year before he finished this order.

And it was all Gabriella Santini's fault.

One day. She'd been in his workshop one day, an hour at most, and he couldn't shake off the memory of her being in his space. She'd looked so interested as she'd roamed the room, careful not touch any of his tools. Usually when people complimented him on his work, he found it easy to shrug their words off as polite praise. But Gabriella's delight in his talent had warmed a cold spot deep within his soul. Her smile had been bright and eager when she'd suggested he use her as a test student for making hooks. At that moment, he would have agreed to damn near anything she asked of him.

He didn't like it, not one bit. And he damn sure didn't want her spending more time in his workshop, intruding on his privacy, crowding his patience. Telling him, not with words but with her brown eyes bold and inviting, that she was open to the possibility of them becoming . . . something.

He couldn't, for the life of him, come up with a reason to tell her it wasn't a good idea for her to be here. And trying to was killing his concentration. Moving over to the work table, he put away his tools and unused pieces of iron and steel. Since he couldn't keep his mind on his work, he'd drive over to Judson's and give him a hand with the horses. Maybe a little exercise would do the trick.

Hanging up his apron, he walked over to the entry just as an

SUV parked in front of the workshop. Through the windshield, he saw Gabriella smile.

"I know," she called out with a laugh in her voice. "It's getting to be a habit, a bad one you think, for me to come without calling first. But I couldn't resist." She walked around to open the back tailgate. It wasn't until she came his way, carrying a black planter holding a small tree with red bows, that he could move.

"I've got it," she said, when he shifted to take it from her.

"What is it?"

"I was at the florist, Buds and Blossoms. Do you know it?" she asked, as if he'd never seen the storefront before. He nodded rather than admit he'd never needed to buy flowers for anyone. "I ordered wreaths for the clinic windows and the outside door leading up to the apartment." She blew out a big breath after she set the tree down on the left side of the entrance. "Mary tried to sell me a small tabletop tree for the apartment, but I want something bigger." She smiled up at him. "Even though it'll take up too much room and I'll have to buy ornaments. But—" She held out her hands and shrugged. "What's Christmas without a tree?"

He looked at the one she'd put by his door. "And so you got me one?"

"Actually, I got you two."

"Two?"

He stood still while she went back to her truck, appearing with another tree. "Just as I was leaving, I saw three of these. There's only room on the clinic porch for one." She set this one down on the right side of the door, stepped back and considered them. "Even if you're not interested in the town business decorating contest, it never hurts to show some holiday spirit. Then, if you want, in the spring, you can plant them." She smiled up at him. "I know it was presumptuous of me, but I wanted to give you something to thank you for helping me make the hooks for my papa."

It was too much—her generosity combined with her honest enjoyment of the task, as well as the fact that nobody had ever thought enough about him to bother. She was giving him a gift of appreciation that also made him feel like a part of the community. Basically, she'd literally brought Christmas to his door.

Her smile and the bright gleam in her gaze were more than he could resist.

He didn't grab her, didn't rush the moment. He took his time, giving her the chance to guess his intention and reject or accept. And allowing him to draw out the anticipation, to make sure he didn't frighten her with the strength of his need.

He kept his touch light as he reached for her and drew her close. She kept her gaze level with his as her hands settled at his waist. He felt the give of her breasts against his chest, the heat of her body as it nestled between his legs. He coasted his hands up and down her back before rising to become lost in her hair. He swore he'd release her if she backed away. He felt her breath catch as he lowered his mouth, his eyes on hers.

He had a moment, an instant only, to stop, to maybe just brush his lips over her cheek. It felt as if time stood still for that brief second. He could hear the distant chirps of a chickadee, could feel the cold of the snow battle the heat of the workshop seeping out of the building. He caught her scent, something dark with promises. And made it impossible to resist any longer.

His lips touched hers.

Hers were soft, mobile as they accepted, opened, invited. He held control a little longer, taking small tastes of her unique flavor, enjoying the way her mouth felt pressed to his. He pushed one hand through her hair, while moving the other to cup her head and hold her in place.

His tongue plunged.

Moans, his and hers, echoed in the stillness. Her hands tightened almost painfully at his waist before they slid to his back, rising to his shoulders. She moved closer, held him tighter.

There was no shyness, no reserve. If he'd hoped to warn her away with the force of his desire, he'd misjudged her badly. Her mouth encouraged him to take more, to give more. And he happily obliged, savoring the sweetness of knowing he'd aroused this passionate woman.

Still hungry for more, he continued to kiss her, to hold her and imagine how her body would look in his bed, her hair spread out on his pillow. When she angled her hips into his, he hissed out a breath.

"No," he groaned, his mouth continuing to take from hers. "Don't move."

"Van." With a sigh, she kissed him again, long and deep. "We have to stop." Her hands moved to his chest. "Please." In defiance of her declaration, her mouth stayed on his a little longer before she finally turned her head so his lips brushed her cheek. She drew in a long breath.

He moved to step back, only her hands fisted in his shirt kept him close. Gently she lowered her forehead to his chest. Without thought, he stroked up and down her spine, as they both struggled to catch their breath.

"I won't apologize," he said.

"Oh, God." Her laughter was hoarse, and her body vibrated with a restraint he admired and cursed as her hands opened and closed on his shirt. "I hope not."

A moment ago, she'd been a hot ball of energy in his arms. Now she seemed fragile and vulnerable.

He really wished he didn't like the way she burrowed into his chest quite so much.

Temptation, desire, pleasure, were all acceptable. They could be dealt with, then put aside. Until they rose again and demanded satisfaction.

It was the longing, the tenderness, the sweetness of holding her that worried him. He closed his eyes, fighting against the rage of wanting what he couldn't have. She was so soft and inviting in his arms, softer than anything he'd ever known. For a second, he indulged in the fantasy that it could be like this again. Always.

But he'd known better, since the first time she caught his eye.

"If I'd suspected I'd get that kind of reaction," she said, "I would have gone for the bigger trees."

No one was more surprised than Van when he laughed. Gabriella leaned back and smiled at him. Then, as if she'd done it a hundred times before, and would do it again another hundred, she rose on her toes and lightly kissed him.

"Thank you for accepting my gift." She stepped back. "Will you get the one for your house from the high school or will you chop one down?"

"I don't have a tree." When she stared at him, he shrugged. "It's just me. Not worth the time or effort."

Her eyes filled with sympathy, the kind of look he'd received in his past that often cut deeper than contempt or doubt. "That's just sad, Van."

"It's the way it's always been. I don't have the kind of family you talk about, Gabriella. I never have."

"Why do I have the feeling you're trying to warn me about something?"

"I get that you're homesick, especially with the holidays coming." He swept out a hand, indicating the small trees she'd delivered. "That's the kind of thing you'd been raised to expect, to do. I'm not like that. You're a doctor, a surgeon. I'm not like any of the men you knew in Chicago." He held out his hands, big hands that reflected the hard line of his work.

"You think I think less of you because you work with your hands?" She threw hers into the air, and spun on her heel. He heard her swearing, at least he figured that's what it was. In Italian.

"You're damned right you're not like any of the men I knew in Chicago. Do you know why I came to Burton Springs?"
"To fill in for Doctor Leonard."

"I came to run away." Her eyes closed as she muttered something in Italian again. She lifted her hands, then let them fall as she looked at him.

"I was involved with someone in Chicago, another doctor, someone I thought I knew, understood. Someone I thought I had a future with. It ended badly. He was on staff while I completed my orthopedics rotation. That's why he insisted we needed to keep our affair quiet, private. It ended when he announced his engagement to a nurse he'd been seeing, the whole time he'd been sleeping with me. A nurse whose father is Chief of Orthopedics. They announced their engagement in front of the hospital staff."

She held her breath, searched for composure and strength even as she was unable to prevent tears from gathering in her eyes.

"It was horrible. I had to go through the motions of being pleased and happy with the news, when all I wanted to do was scream ."

Van couldn't stop the flare of jealousy. She'd been in love with someone else. He could see the loss of that love in her eyes, in the reflection of the tears she struggled to keep from falling. She'd come to Montana to escape the pain, the man, and the memories.

"Needless to say, I was shocked to hear of the engagement," she continued. "I had no idea the rat bastard was two-timing me. God. It was lowering to realize how foolish I'd been. But I soon realized that my pride was more crushed than my heart." Anger slipped through a small crack in her composure.

"I was angry at him, yes, but more so at myself."

"Why?"

"I'd trusted him, and he lied to me." Van stood stock still and said nothing. "No sooner had the engagement been announced than I left the hospital and went home." Her chest rose and fell as her breathing accelerated. "He came to see me later that night. Can you believe the arrogance?"

"Did you slam the door in his face?"

Her lips curved, slightly. "Unfortunately, I'd given him a key so he breezed right in. He was genuinely shocked that I wouldn't let him touch me. He thought we'd continue as we had before the announcement of his engagement." She threw her hands out, as if she now held the guy off. "Not only did I tell him no, *absolutely never* would he again put hands on me, but I made the mistake of wondering aloud what his new fiancée would say—along with her father—if they learned he'd been involved with someone else while dating her." Her eyes darkened. "That's when he shoved me against the wall and threatened me."

Van moved within reach of her, his hands closing into fists at his side. "He touched you?"

He'd grown up with violence. For as long as he could remember, he'd known the brutal pain of a fist. He knew what it felt like to fly in the air as you were tossed aside, slammed into a wall. To have your cry cut short because a hand wrapped around your throat, squeezing until you passed out. Waking up bruised and hurting in spirit as much as body. Questioning why the hell you shouldn't find a way to end your life before he did.

"How did you get rid of him?"

"Every woman's best defense. I kneed him in the crotch."

In spite of the hurt he heard lingering in her voice, he chuckled. And hoping to improve her mood more, he shifted his stance a little to the side. He was rewarded with her strained laugh.

"So, yes, Van, you're nothing like the men I knew in Chicago." She reached for his hands. "From where I'm standing, that's a very good thing."

"That's not saying much if you're comparing me to that idiot you just talked about."

"I'm saying it because you are a good man. I'll admit, we haven't known each other long, but we have friends in common. I know they like you. You're talented, you're respected and admired by your community." She tilted her head a little and stared at him.

"This is new territory for me, Van. I've never become involved with someone so quickly, especially with an end date in sight." His hands jerked in hers, but she kept a grip on him. "But I want you to know, whatever choices we make during the next few weeks, I trust you."

GABRIELLA AVOIDED Van for the next two days. She'd shocked him with her blatant offer. Granted she had little experience with this kind of non-relationship intimacy, but that wasn't what had her staying away.

She'd come to the realization that more than she wanted

him as a lover, she wanted him as a friend.

Never would she forget the stunned realization, and reluctant acceptance, of her bringing him such a small gift . . . followed by the hollow tone of his voice when he said he wasn't worth the time or effort of having a Christmas tree.

Because she'd been raised in a loving family, she recognized someone who hadn't known that blessing. He hadn't said more, but she'd seen the way he stood still when she explained about Timothy shoving her against the wall. The way his hands had closed into fists.

Van had known violence in his past.

She wasn't sure if he'd been on the receiving end of it, or if he'd had to learn to control his temper. Then she remembered the way he'd held a frightened little girl and she knew in her heart that his anger wasn't the problem. She'd told him she trusted him, and she did, as far as knowing he'd never intentionally hurt or betray her. She wanted his trust in return. She wanted him to know that he could tell her anything and it wouldn't alter her respect for the man she was coming to know.

"And avoiding him isn't the way to earn that trust," she whispered while closing the patient chart she'd been updating.

She forwarded clinic calls to her cell, and ran a few errands before driving out to Van's place. Wanting the connection, she used her Bluetooth to call home. "Mama," she said, thrilled when her mother answered the phone.

"Gabriella," Dr. Noelle Santini said. She didn't know how her mother did it, but there was a wealth of love and pleasure in the greeting. "What a wonderful treat. I took the afternoon off. I was just waiting for your daddy to come home after the lunch rush. We're having an afternoon movie date. He'll be sad that he missed you." Gabriella could picture her mother's smile. In spite of the long hours in both their careers, her parents made the effort to have this kind of alone time.

"And what are your plans?" her mother asked. "I know you are in the car. Are you going to see another of your interesting patients?"

"No."

"Gabriella?" her mother asked when she remained silent. "Is something wrong?"

"I'm going to see a friend, Mama. A man. He's helping me make Papa something for Christmas."

A pause. "Is he just a friend?"

"For now. Mama, I want what you have, what you and Papa have together. The love and respect, the trust, the family."

"There is nothing I would wish more for you."

"Then why am I considering being intimate with a man when I know there's no future?"

"Perhaps that is part of the allure?"

"I was so wrong before. With Timothy."

"No." The denial cut sharp like a warmed knife through butter. Her mother swore, using the two Italian phrases she knew. And still, after almost forty years of marriage, she mangled them. "You were right. He was the one who was wrong."

"Mama, of course you take my side."

"I take your side, yes, because I love you, but also because he wasn't honest with you. This man, the one you're thinking of now, is he honest?"

Gabriella thought of her suspicion about his past. Then she thought of his character, the respect the community had for him. She recalled that fierce light in his eyes when she told him about Timothy shoving her. She warmed at the thought of the way he'd held her, kissed her. When she'd asked him to stop, he'd done so without pause, question or insult.

"Yes, he is."

"I trust you," her mother said, bringing tears to Gabriella's eyes. "But I want you to promise me something."

"Anything."

"Don't be afraid. Trust yourself. Trust your heart."

Her mother's words repeated in her mind as she parked in front of Van's workshop. For a second she simply sat, considered, debated. Until the urgent tugging in the pit of her stomach was too strong to resist.

Her gaze lingered on the trees she'd delivered. Unable to resist, she pressed a fingertip to the soil, discovered it damp.

Pleased he was tending the plants, and hoping she could convince him to set up a Christmas tree inside his house, she stepped forward. Then she noticed that both doors were closed.

"Van?" Her call and knock went unanswered. "Well, hell. That's what I get for not calling ahead."

She went back to her car for some paper. She'd written half her note when she caught a glimpse of something moving. Her breath caught in her throat.

Coming over the hill at the rear of his place, Van rode a horse at an easy pace. A trot she thought it was called. He looked like something out of a western movie, with his cowboy hat tugged low on his brow, his gloved hands holding the reins, his jeans snug on his muscular thighs. His head lifted, his gaze zeroing in on her when the dog running alongside him barked and sprinted ahead.

Gabriella moved to the other side of the car, braced against the side as she waited to see what the German shepherd would do. It charmed her by stopping inches from her boots and sitting back on his haunches.

"You have a dog?"

"She's not mine." Van dismounted, tying the reins to the workshop porch railing. "This is Ginger, she belongs to Judson Ford. He's delivering a string of horses and . . ." She was surprised to see him look down at his boots as a faint blush rose on his cheeks. "Uhm, well, he's meeting someone."

"I think I understand," she said, smiling.

"I told Judson that Ginger could stay here with me. She won't bite."

Bending over, she offered her hand, charmed yet again when the dog nudged her palm with her head. "Oh, aren't you a sweet one?" she said, stroking her hand over the soft fur.

"You like dogs?"

"I don't know." She smiled up at Van as he walked over. "Between my parents' hours at their respective jobs and my brother's sports commitments, we weren't home much." She shrugged. "It just didn't seem fair to have a dog and keep it inside for long periods of time."

"You didn't play sports?"

She laughed and sank both hands deep into Ginger's fur. "I was your typical bookworm, concentrating on my studies. How about you?"

"No."

She straightened at the curt reply, at the reminder there were secrets he had yet to trust her with. Trust came in many forms. Right now, she offered hers by not pushing for answers or explanations. The dog moved over to the porch to lap at a large metal bowl of water.

"Does the horse belong to Judson too?" He nodded. "Ever think of getting your own?"

"I tell myself I don't need one." He looked around. "There's no reason for me to have one."

"Maybe if you're a good boy, Santa will bring you one. Besides—" she continued when he snorted out a mocking laugh. Maybe she had outgrown belief in a fantasy gift-giver, but she would always cling to the belief in the magic of the holiday season. "Wouldn't the pleasure it would give you be reason enough?"

He turned back to her, his gaze taking a long heart-pounding survey. "You're wearing jeans." Not even the shielding brim of his hat could hide the seductive glint in his eye. "They look good on you."

Her throat went dry, making it necessary to swallow once before she could speak. "I was hoping we could start work on the hooks. You said I needed to wear jeans and not a dress." She rubbed a hand over the denim. "Once again, I apologize for not calling before I drove out. I know you have work that needs to be finished before Christmas."

His hand closed over hers, and he tugged so she stumbled into his embrace. "Have you changed your mind?" His mouth skimmed hers before he moved to linger at the spot just below her ear.

"Changed my mind?" she repeated, wondering how she could change her mind when it had gone completely blank.

"About being here." His mouth nipped at the exposed line

of her jaw before moving to press against the rapid pulse at her throat. "About being with me."

"No."

"Then come with me now."

She blinked as he stepped back. Without his warmth, without the thrill of his mouth skimming over her skin, she now felt the cold. Dazed, she watched his hand appear before her, an invitation impossible to resist. She didn't know where he planned to take them. It didn't matter. Trust, she thought as she slipped her hand into his, came in many phases. She *did* trust him, more than should be possible in so short a time. She'd go wherever he led.

Even so, when they stepped onto the workshop porch, she felt her body relax. She may have decided she wanted to be intimate with him, and the dwindling time they had together loomed large, but she hadn't been prepared to go to bed with him today. Apparently he felt the same way.

"You've taken care of the trees," she said as he slid open the left door, flicked up switches to turn on lights. The dog entered with them, crossing to settle down on a cushion beneath the workbench.

"They're evergreens, they pretty much take care of themselves."

She looked around the room marveling, as she'd done the last time she'd been here, the delicacy of some of the items. "Once again," she said, running a fingertip along the curved metal legs of a tall curvy sculpture holding an elongated lantern at the top. "I'm impressed with the fluid look of what you create." She traced several of the multiple, interlocking and twining strands rising out of the wider base. "It's graceful and flowing. Sensual."

"The client wanted something unique for the lighting on their outdoor patio."

"You've given them beauty along with function." Her gaze lifted to his. "It takes patience, strength and vision to accomplish what you've built here," she said. "The business as much as the individual pieces."

"Those are pretty words, Doc. But there's a world of difference between what we do." He paused, reaching for one solid point of argument. "Between the kind of people we are."

"You think so?" She took a long look around the shop before locking her gaze on his. "I see a man who has a talent for the work he's chosen, who takes pride in that work. And the town obviously recognizes and appreciates your talent." She smiled when he stared at her. "I've been told you're making the topper for the Christmas tree in the center of town."

"The mayor didn't give me the option of saying no."

"She has a way of getting what she wants." Gabriella leaned forward, her tongue tucked in her cheek. "What did you make?"

"I'm not showing you." His brows bunched in a frown as he shrugged out of his coat. "Did she ask you to check up on me?"

"No. Why would you think that?"

"She said something about having a committee member get in touch." He pointed at the wall. "After you take off your coat, put on that apron hanging there. And you'll need to wear gloves." He held those out. "Since we'll be working together, we'll each wear one. It'll be big on you, but you need to protect your hand."

Van began by telling her names and purposes of the tools they'd be using—the forge for heating the iron so it was malleable, hammers for forming the shape of the rods, and the anvil to balance the rod and to help form the shape. He selected three rods, all the same length and width, then handed one to her.

"We'll start by heating the tip. Just put the end into the forge." He stood close, his uncovered hand curling around her wrist as he showed her how deep to put it in. "See how the tip's turning orange? That's how you know it's hot. Now." He guided her hand to settle the glowing rod on the anvil. "Use the hammer to pound out this end to a point. Hit it hard," he said with a chuckle at the light tap she gave it. "It's iron. You're not going to hurt it."

"I'm not as strong as you are."

"I don't believe that. When I first started, it helped to think of someone I wanted to punch. Then I was able to pound it hard."

"Who did you think of?" she asked as she lifted the hammer and thought of Timothy. She felt the energy sing up her arm when it connected with the iron.

"Too many to name."

"That's just sad, Van." Sympathy made her second blow softer, less effective.

"Tell me something I don't know. Something I didn't live," he added under his breath. But her hearing was excellent. "Good," he commented, lifting the rod to examine her work after she'd taken a couple more swings. His eyes were amused when he looked at her. "Guess you thought of someone after all."

"Yes, I did," she said, knowing he wouldn't want to hear that she'd been thinking of all the people in his past who'd hurt him.

"Now, the next one."

"But this one doesn't look like a hook."

"It's best to forge in stages when making multiples. It makes them more uniform and it saves time with less tool exchange."

After she finished the first stage of the last hook, he guided her through the process of placing the tip over the horn of the anvil and gently taping the end so it curled into an open U shape. Then she used the hammer to flatten the opposite end into a broad spot where, once the iron cooled, holes for hanging would be drilled. The heat of the forge caused a trail of sweat to roll down between her breasts. And the heat of having Van cradled behind her, his arms firm around her, his hands sure and steady on hers, had a fire building in her belly. And below.

"Why don't you take a break?" he suggested, stepping back. "I'll finish this last part."

He lifted a tool that resembled her papa's favorite meat cleaver, using it with the same skill hacking at iron that Papa used in cutting meat, as he sliced the flattened end of the hook away from the rest of the iron rod.

She let her gaze travel over him. She knew that his chest,

while hard, could offer comfort as it embraced. The muscles in his arms would be a delight to trace and explore. Her body vibrated with the wish to be caressed by those strong, capable hands.

"I never realized blacksmithing could feel so erotic."

The oath rang out harsh and loud. In shock and horror, she looked down to see her words had caused his hand to jerk.

The blade of the tool had sliced across his uncovered palm.

"*Mi dispiace.* I'm sorry," she repeated in English, shaking off her glove and clamping her fingers on his wrist so he couldn't move. She'd trained for years on how to deal with blood and trauma, even though this was the first time she'd been the cause of the wound. The dog whined as she crossed the room to press against Van's leg. "It's okay, girl," Gabriella soothed, scratching behind the dog's ears. "After I clean the wound, I'll determine whether or not you need stitches."

Now some of his color drained away. She couldn't help being amused at the panic in his eyes. "You're a big, strong man who gets his palm sliced open with a wicked looking tool, and you don't flinch. But at the thought of a needle prick, you're about to pass out?"

"No needles."

"At the very least, you'll need a shot to prevent infection," she said. Looking into his eyes she saw no sign of shock, but there was something there, some dark shadow from his past. "You work with your hands. We can't risk compromising your mobility."

"You didn't give that little girl a shot."

Pausing by her vehicle, she grabbed her medical bag. "A small rooster peck is a far cry from a slice from a used tool." She pushed down on the lever handle in the same design as the finely wrought iron inlay on the door she'd admired on her first visit, and shoved it open.

What she'd assumed was the front door she learned was in fact the back door, leading into the kitchen. Seeing it now, she admitted it made sense for him to have it face his shop in this way, and use this entrance after a long day of work.

"Convenient," she said, nodding to the left where she spotted a combination laundry/bathroom, complete with a shower.

"Practical," he said. "I can strip off when I come inside and throw my clothes into the washer."

"Hmmm." With that image playing havoc with her pulse, she settled him in the largest chair of the mismatched four circling the round wooden table. "Alright," she said, opening her bag. "Trust me, Van. You won't even feel the needle." She smiled. "After all, it's almost Christmas, the best time for miracles."

Chapter Four

VAN SAT STILL while Gabriella moved around his kitchen. But his mind bounced from one thought to another.

So far, none of those thoughts had focused on the needle prick she promised. On the other hand, a quick jab would be over and done with. He had a gut feeling what he felt for her was going to stay a lot longer.

"We'll start with this," she said, placing towels alongside a bowl of steaming water in front of him. She sat, reached for his hand and began to unravel the towel she'd used to stop the blood flow. Her hands were steady and soothing.

"This will sting a little," she cautioned, sinking his hand into the water. He sucked in a breath between his teeth. "Sorry, but we have to make sure it's clean before I apply antiseptic and stitch it."

Sweat popped out on his forehead at the mention of the needle.

She ran her hands over his, soaping, rinsing, drying with a clean towel. She held his aloft, studying the wound before tenderly laying it on another clean towel. Still, she wrapped her fingers around his wrist. When she looked at him, he saw the concern. *"Scusi."*

"What?" he asked.

"I'm so sorry." She searched his face, her gaze taking in the sweat beading on his forehead. "This is my fault."

"I'm the one who wasn't paying attention." And he hadn't been. At her declaration that working beside him was erotic, his mind had filled with sensual images. He cleared his throat, hoped like hell she couldn't see the nerves bouncing inside of him. "If you're really sorry, you could change your mind about that needle and thread."

She probed at his palm a little but smiled when her gaze met his. "You'll be happy to know I don't think stitches will be necessary. The cut doesn't go very deep." She reached into her bag, drew out a sealed package. He could see the vial and needle.

He instinctively tried to pull away, but she stopped him. "You said no stitches."

"When was the last time you had a tetanus shot?" He shook his head—he didn't have a clue. "Then this is a good precaution." She opened the package, snapped on some gloves. He looked just over the top of her head, felt a small pinch. "See? Not so bad."

He looked down, watched as she spread a generous amount of antiseptic cream over the wound. "You'll need to keep this as dry as possible. I have some gloves I can give you to use." She wrapped a gauze bandage around the wound. Then, as she'd done with the little girl at Evergreen, she leaned down and pressed her lips to his palm. "I'm so glad I'm not responsible for you missing any work."

"I've lived through worse."

"That doesn't make me feel better."

She gathered up everything she'd used and tucked it all inside her bag. Then she took the bowl of water back to the sink.

"I can do that," he said, when she ran the water and squirted soap in the bowl.

"Keep it dry as much as possible," she repeated.

He didn't want the image of her at the sink, looking far too much at home, in his mind. It made him wish for things he couldn't have. Temptation, desire, pleasure, were all acceptable. They could be dealt with, then put aside. Until they rose again and demanded satisfaction.

She'd made it clear she was interested in them getting to know each other *much* better. He could hardly lie and say he didn't want to be with her. It was the longing that caught him by the throat that worried him.

"You should be able to work, provided you're careful and wear latex gloves to prevent infecting the wound," Gabriella said, turning to lean back against the sink. "I think it's best if you take it easy the rest of today."

"I have to get the horse back to Judson's."

"Van, I'm not sure that's smart. The shot I gave you is relatively mild but there's a chance you might have a reaction. You could become dizzy and fall off the horse."

"So ride with me."

Van nearly bit his tongue in half the instant the words out of his mouth. He knew he could ride the damn horse with no problem. He had no business asking Gabriella to come along. To have her sitting in the saddle, pressed against him, his arms around her as the pretense for making sure she didn't slide off. Only now, with the idea planted firmly in his mind, he couldn't regret the suggestion.

"Are you out of your mind?" Her arms lifted as her hands slashed through the air. "Two of us on a horse?" Her hands made another slashing motion as she muttered under her breath. In Italian. He had absolutely no idea what she'd said but he could hear the passion in her voice. And soon, he hoped, he'd experience that passion in his bed.

"What's the matter, Gabriella? Afraid?"

She tossed up her chin, and narrowed her gaze. "I've worked hours in the emergency room, have seen just about every kind of harm one person can inflict on another." She took two steps toward him. "Because of my training, I've saved lives." She took another two steps, close enough now to jab him in the chest with her finger. "I don't have the luxury of being afraid."

He curled a hand around her finger, kept her close. "Then ride with me."

Her eyes darkened with the unintended double meaning of his words. He lifted her hand, kissing the fingertip as gently as she'd kissed his palm.

"At least if we fall off, I'll be able to say I told you so," she said.

"Have a little faith."

"I'm going to need more than a little." Freeing her hand, she made the Catholic sign of the cross. "So how does this work?" she asked, as they walked outside. Before leaving the kitchen, she'd tucked her cell phone into the pocket of her coat.

Van untied the reins of the horse, then walked him into a clearing. At his feet, Ginger quivered with the knowledge she'd soon be allowed to run free.

"I've got the reins," he said, pulling them over the horse's head. "Hold onto the horn and put your left foot in the stirrup. Let your weight rest on the ball of your foot. That's it. Now swing your other leg over the top. Don't grab the back of the saddle," he warned. "Settle down nice and slow. Scoot forward a little, again nice and slow. There you go. You're doing fine."

"Now what?"

He bit back a smile, seeing the white knuckles on the hand she had wrapped around the saddle horn. "Now take both of your feet out of the stirrups."

"What? Why?" But she did what he asked.

"So I can do this." He put his foot in the stirrup and swung up behind her. The horse sidestepped a little at the extra weight but with a pull on the reins, he settled down. Gabriella felt as sweet leaning back against his chest as he'd imagined she'd be.

"How does a blacksmith know all this horse stuff?"

"Pretty much the same way I know about blacksmith stuff. I picked it up as I went along."

The silence was relaxed, which mainly meant that she didn't ask any questions he wasn't ready to answer. Ginger ran ahead of them, stopping every so often to look back, making sure they were following.

Then the silence exploded with a shot.

"What was that?" Gabriella asked. Van clamped an arm around her middle, holding her still, keeping the horse calm.

"Shotgun."

"Cosa hai detto."

"English," Van said, chuckling a little.

"Oh, sorry. Basically, I asked you to explain."

He shifted the horse so they faced a stand of trees. "See that truck?" She nodded, her hair brushing against his cheek. "Someone from the high school is shooting mistletoe out of the upper branches of the tree. They always have some for sale at the

Christmas tree lot."

"Shooting it out of the tree," she echoed. "Really?"

"See?" Two people appeared from between the trees, carrying large bundles in each hand that they then placed in the truck bed. Van guided the horse around so they could resume the ride. "Usually, by this time of year, most of the mistletoe on the lower branches has been eaten by moose, elk and deer. Even squirrels and some birds eat the berries."

"Oh," she said as they crested a hill, her breath a white cloud in the cold air. "Look at that sweet cabin."

"That belongs to Nicholas Anderson. Judson gave it to Nicholas. This is Judson's land."

"Is he a relative?"

"No, he was one of Judson's high school teachers, who helped him get a scholarship for college."

"That's right. I remember Judson mentioning he'd lived in Chicago for a while. Small world."

"On the night of the tree lighting, he dresses like Santa for the kids."

"Nicholas or Judson?"

He laughed, she always made him laugh. "Nicholas."

"A man named Nicholas, posing as Santa. It's perfect."

She angled so she could grin at him over her shoulder. Her face, her mouth, was right there. It felt natural and easy to lean forward for a quick kiss.

"Judson brings horses and a wagon of some kind for rides." He kissed her again. "Will you go for a ride with me?"

"I'd love to."

ON THE DAY before Thanksgiving, Gabriella drove to the high school. She needed something to keep her busy, to keep her from dwelling on the tearful phone conversation she'd had with her mother last night, one that had been a poor substitute for their annual night together. Under the string of lights around the Christmas tree lot, she spent an hour examining and considering before finally choosing the tree she wanted for the apartment. She paid, adding a generous tip for delivery on Friday, then chatted with other people looking for the perfect tree. And afterwards, she bought and enjoyed a cup of hot cider before driving to The Market.

She might have been able to do her shopping and go back to the apartment without pause, only she drew up short at the end of an aisle. Midway down, a little girl laughed with delight as her mother tossed a box of macaroni and cheese into their cart. Gabriella stood there, frozen with longing. If she'd been in Chicago, she and her mother would have chased the men of the family out of the house before sharing the one dish her mother knew how to cook—mac and cheese— followed by snuggling under blankets on the sofa with popcorn to watch movies.

They could have done all of that tonight, via FaceTime, but they'd both decided they didn't want that poor substitute. Instead, they'd promised to clear their schedules and have their night once she was back home after the first of the year. Still, it hurt to watch the happy family, and her stomach cramped. As she stood there watching the mother and daughter walk away, Van rounded the corner.

"What's wrong?" he asked, stepping forward, obviously seeing her distress.

"You caught me at a low moment. I'm not used to being alone at this time of year." Then she proceeded to tell him more than he'd likely intended to hear. Finally realizing it wasn't doing her any good to dwell on what she was missing, she pointed at the packages he held. "Rolls?"

"Everyone wants rolls on Thanksgiving." He glanced at the contents of her cart.

"Van." She clamped a hand on his arm. "Come home with me."

"Now?"

"Yes." She might have laughed at his question if not for the inviting gleam that darkened his eyes. He knew what she wanted, and obviously wanted the same thing. She knew she wanted him in her bed. So why not tonight?

But she wasn't quite ready to say that yet. "Come to my apartment. Let me cook you dinner." Her hand closed once, relaxed. "There's no reason we both have to be alone tonight. Please," she said when he hesitated, glancing around. She noticed people watching them.

"I don't know if this is a good idea."

His protest was ruined by the distinct rumbling of his stomach. With glee, she pushed a fingertip into his belly. "I've got one or two more items to pick up. Come over whenever you're ready." Then she smiled, turned, and walked away.

BY TIME SHE heard the knock on the downstairs door, Gabriella had sauce simmering and water on a low boil for the spaghetti . . . from a box. "*Mi scusi*, Papa," she said, hurrying down the steps to throw open the door.

"*Benvenuto.* Welcome. Come in out of the cold."

Before she could second-guess herself, she settled her hands on his shoulders and kissed his cheeks. "Mistletoe," she said, looking above where they stood. "I bought some when I picked out my Christmas tree. And yes, they told me it was from where we heard them shooting it down."

Backing away, she ran a suddenly damp palm over her apron. "Hang your coat there." She pointed at a wall rack where her winter coat hung next to her white lab coat. "Then come on up." Not giving him a chance to tell her he'd changed his mind, she climbed the stairs.

"I had to make do with pre-made meatballs," she said, once she sensed his presence behind her. As with the boxed pasta, her papa would have been disappointed. With Van there, the small room that she'd always thought of as cozy now felt confining. And she was more aware than ever that her bed was separated from the kitchen and living room combination by a thin privacy screen. Taking a deep breath, she turned, holding a glass of red wine in each hand.

He shook his head before she could offer him one. "I don't drink."

"Oh." She set the glasses down, then moved to the refrigerator. "I have sparkling water." At his nod, she drew out a bottle and poured some water into a goblet.

"Thanks." He drank deep as she leaned back against the counter and sipped her wine. "My father was a drunk," he admitted. "A mean one. No—" he said when she moved to set down her glass. "I don't want you to do anything different."

She searched his face, saw the hard lines of determination along with those of past pain. She'd wanted his trust and he'd given her a small sample of it now. She'd do nothing to jeopardize him giving her more. So she took another deliberate sip of wine and waited.

"He was some kind of big deal football player in high school, good enough to get a scholarship. Only during the first week of summer practice, he blew out his knee. He left school, came home, got his girlfriend pregnant. They got married and he got a job working at the local bottling factory. He and his buddies liked to stop at a neighborhood bar after their shift before heading home. Some nights he came home and slept off the booze."

"Other nights," she softly said when he grew quiet. "He didn't?"

"Your water's boiling." He avoided her gaze by taking a drink.

Gabriella juggled the disappointment of him ending the conversation with the desire to give him a night free of troubled memories. Wasn't getting her mind off her loneliness one of the reasons she'd invited him?

"Would you mind slicing the bread?" she asked, nodding to where a crusty loaf, a knife and a cutting board sat on the counter. She slid the spaghetti from box to pot, then stirred the sauce she'd managed to make in the short time she'd had. "Here." She scooped up spoonful, blew to cool it down, and held it out to him. "What do you think?"

He kept his gaze locked on hers as he took a taste. Pride burst in her when his eyes widened in pleasure. "How did you do all this in so short a time?"

"My papa owns a restaurant. I've spent many a night helping either in the kitchen or waiting tables. I've learned to work fast."

"I'm sorry."

"No, I enjoyed it." She turned down the heat on the pot. "That's not what I meant."

Before she could ask him to explain, he pulled her close and tight . . . and took her mouth. She tasted the tang of tomato sauce, the spice of garlic, basil and crushed red pepper he'd just tried. But aside from that, she tasted Van. Her mind swirling, a moan escaped.

"I'm pretty sure this isn't something you and your mother usually do tonight," he said against her lips before taking the kiss deeper.

"Van."

"Oh, no." He released her, then stepped back and smiled in a way that had her heart skipping. "You're not getting out of feeding me now."

HE SMILED MORE, more than she'd ever seen him do so, as they ate and talked. After he helped with the dishes and she made coffee, they settled on the loveseat.

"Where are you going to put a Christmas tree?" he asked.

"The better question is, where will I put all the gifts?"

He ran his thumb up and down the side of his coffee mug. "I bet it's crazy at your house on Christmas morning."

"No, we're very organized. We start with the youngest opening the first gift and move on one at a time." She rubbed a fist at the ache in her chest.

"It must take forever."

"Christmas is only one day. We like to make it last." Tentative, she sipped her coffee. "What about you? What traditions did your family have?"

"We never got many gifts. My mother used to like the presents my sister and I managed to make." He shrugged. "Colored pictures when we were little. The year Rosie learned to crochet, she made a scarf for each of us."

"Is your sister younger or older?"

"Younger."

Her throat closed at the pain of loss she heard in his voice. She waited, but when he offered nothing else, she decided she didn't need to hear anymore tonight. She wanted him to relax and laugh. So she braced her back against the arm of the love seat, and nudged his thigh with her bare foot. Her breath caught in her throat when his big warm hand curled around her ankle and kept her foot against him.

"Does this mean you'll take Mama's place and paint my nails?" she asked, batting her eyelashes as if the idea amused her.

"Sure."

She laughed, tried to move away. But he held her still. "Van, I was kidding."

"You think I can't do it."

"I'm sure you can."

He leaned over the short distance separating them. She could smell coffee on his breath, could see the hesitancy reflected in his green eyes. "I haven't racked up too many good memories in my lifetime. Maybe next year, when you're with your mother again, you'll think of this one. And me." To her delight, he smiled as he sat back. "Besides, maybe it'll stop you from suggesting we watch some chick flick."

"Wrong." She laughed as she stood. "I'm very good at multi-tasking. Be right back."

She rounded the corner of the privacy screen, paused and closed her eyes. How was she supposed to resist him when he was like this? Relaxed. Sexy as hell. She didn't want to fall for him. She couldn't. She'd be leaving in a few short weeks.

She drew in a deep breath and opened her eyes. She'd never allowed anyone or anything to change the direction of her life. And she wasn't about to start now, regardless of how tempted she was by Van.

Somehow, she'd find a way to keep him from getting anywhere near her heart.

"OH, YOU PUT up your tree already." Gabriella stood in the doorway of Carter and Audra's ranch house, not sure whether to enter the warm, welcoming kitchen first, or the large, inviting family room, where their two oldest boys were playing with cars, trucks, and action figures beneath the low branches of a still-bare Christmas tree. She'd been the first guest to arrive.

"I know it's early," Audra said. "But we've learned to do what we can when we have the boys down for the night."

Gabriella turned in time to see Carter wrap an arm around his wife's waist and whisper something in her ear that made her blush. She didn't think either of them regretted not getting the tree decorated. She shifted back to look at the tree.

"I'm having mine delivered tomorrow," she said. "I just couldn't break tradition and do it before Thanksgiving."

"I'm going out to string the lights on your studio," Carter said to his wife. "Do you want me to take the boys outside and let them run off some steam?"

"No, let's leave them alone while they're quiet," Audra said.

"Won't last."

"I wouldn't have it any other way." Audra smiled.

Once Carter went outside, Gabriella followed Audra into the kitchen to finish putting together her appetizers of stuffed mushrooms along with a cheese tray. Ellen arrived soon after, and immediately got busy in the kitchen. Judson Ford and Rhonda and Sheriff Owens arrived shortly after that. And when Carter finished his outdoor decorating, he came back inside with Kendall and Logan and their two children in tow, with Ryland and Sydney—and Van—right behind them. Gabriella locked eyes with Van, smiling when she spotted the packaged rolls in his hands.

Gone was the relaxed manner that had so charmed her last night. Back was the caution, the reserve of keeping their attraction private. While she appreciated his discretion, she wished he didn't feel he had to act that way. She'd been stung by a hidden relationship once. She wasn't anxious to experience it again. Maybe what she and Van had wouldn't, couldn't, develop into a full-blown relationship, but that didn't mean she had to conceal her feelings.

Her determination last night, not to allow her plans to change, felt a little less firm today. Surrounded by friends, looking forward to the magic of the holidays, appreciating the warmth of a home rooted in love and the attention of an attractive man, she decided to give in to the joy she could have today.

With her hands on his shoulders, she lightly kissed him. "Happy Thanksgiving, Van."

THERE WERE differences, as well as similarities, to the kind of Thanksgivings she'd known with her family. Just like in her father's kitchen, there was conversation, laughter, stealing small bites and samples along with the occasional complaint. Going with the festive mood, and ignoring the discussion about whether or not they were rushing the season, someone turned on Christmas music. Come Monday, she'd follow up on the status of her surgical fellowship—she'd actually put it on her calendar—but for this day, she ignored all thoughts of leaving.

She did, however, keep a close eye on Sydney Evans, who no longer wore the sun-kissed glow of a new bride. Twice, she'd had to practically bolt into the bathroom. Having been told she wasn't needed in the crowded kitchen, Gabriella had planned to corner Sydney when an argument broke out between the kids.

"Marissa Anne," Kendall complained. "I thought you were going to keep your brother and cousins busy."

"They won't listen to me." She pouted. "I want to go outside and see the horses."

"I have an idea," Gabriella said, eyeing the Christmas tree. She looked at Audra's oldest son. "Do you have some construction paper and crayons?"

He rubbed his nose, his eyes miserable, and tilted his head in the direction of the small table and chairs off in a corner of the room. She nodded at Marissa. "I've got this. You go ahead and go outside. Go on," she said when the girl hesitated.

When Marissa realized she was getting a reprieve, she spun on her heel and dashed away, and Gabriella walked over to the little ones. Soon she had them settled at the table, tracing a crayon around their spread hands. When the baby woke from his nap, she blocked Audra from seeing what she had the small boys doing. "I'll get him."

"Oh, but . . ."

Gabriella lifted a brow. "You'll trust me to see to his health but not change his diaper?"

"Well . . ." Audra smiled. "When you put it that way."

"Stay out of here until you're told to come." Audra sent her a questioning look but nodded and returned to the kitchen.

Gabriella spotted Van watching her—not for the first time today—and curled a finger for him to walk her way. "Keep an eye on those boys for a minute, will you?" She explained what they were doing and then hurried up the stairs.

With a changed Beckett snuggled in her arms, she came back down and found Van squatting beside the table, his big hands gently helping smaller kids color and punch holes in the cutout handprints she planned to string with a ribbon as a garland for the tree. The sight stopped her in her tracks.

She had a blessed life, with parents who encouraged, loved and supported her, with so many good memories of a happy childhood, as well as a fantastic relationship with her brothers— back then, and now—and with a career she'd worked long and hard for.

None of that, however, could compete with the image before her, and every longing it triggered. Years from now, she would think back to this day, to the warmth and love of this house, the feel of a baby in her arms. Her strong attraction for a man kind-hearted enough to help some young boys with a craft project for a holiday that didn't hold the same magic and hope for him as it filled within her.

She was very much afraid that image, and possibly the man, was permanently imprinted on her heart.

Chapter Five

THE REST OF THE country might be fighting crowds while Christmas shopping for deals on the Friday after Thanksgiving, but Gabriella's morning involved wrapping an ankle sprain stemming from an impromptu football game, examining and prescribing a new treatment for a teenager suffering with severe acne, and bandaging a hot oil burn on a forearm.

But an hour later, things got much better. "That's perfect," she said as the teenage boy settled her Christmas tree in a corner of the apartment. Digging into the pocket of her lab coat, she drew out the tip she'd offered him to carry the tree upstairs for her.

"It's big," the boy said, pocketing the bill. "Hope you've got plenty of lights and ornaments. Guess you could get some bandages or needles from downstairs, if need be."

She returned his grin. "I'll keep that in mind."

Later that day, with Christmas carols playing on her phone, she strung lights. Because she associated white lights on a Christmas tree with home, she went with colored. This apartment wasn't home. With the lights set on a timer, the ornaments she'd purchased hanging mostly in the front of the tree, and the addition of ribbon she'd bought for gift wrapping, she had a tree that would welcome her home each night.

She was on the clinic front porch signing for the delivery from Buds and Blossoms when Van arrived.

"Hey. You didn't say anything about coming into town today."

"You wanted a tree, didn't you?"

"A tree?" She frowned. "Yes, I had one . . . oh," she said when he lifted a Christmas tree made of horseshoes like the one she'd admired in his workshop. Before she could tell him to bring it inside, he reached back into the truck bed and lifted out another piece.

"Oh, Van. It's wonderful." She stared, ridiculously thrilled by his gift of a horseshoe reindeer, including the red iron ball for a nose. "But maybe we should take it inside to go with the tree. You know, so no one's tempted to make off with it."

"City girl." He placed the reindeer by the door. "No one around here's going to steal it."

"But what about visitors? The mayor's sent out flyers to the surrounding communities about the activities and tree lighting tomorrow."

He grimaced. "Yeah, I know. She tried to get me to say something. I told her no way. I made the topper, that's enough."

"I wish you would."

He straightened, stared at her. "It was her idea."

"It's your work." Leaving it at that, she opened the clinic door, and gestured for him to take the horseshoe tree inside. "This is the second time today I've had a handsome man deliver a Christmas tree. Put it over there, angled in the corner."

Van came back onto the porch and, without asking or making any comment, lifted one of the wreaths she'd bought earlier to the window, gauging where best to pound the nail he fished out of a pocket. They worked together, hanging the wreaths, discussed how best to string the lights. She'd gone with the colored lights to contrast the white of an electronic candle in each window. People stopped by, offering compliments or suggestions. Van took three orders from shop owners for the horseshoe reindeer for next year's displays.

"Well," she said, stepping off the porch to give it a long look once they were done. "It won't win any decorating contests, but it'll do." She slipped her phone out of a pocket and took several pictures to send to her family. "Move over by the reindeer. Come on," she pleaded when he shook his head. "It'll be a nice shot for your website." She lowered the phone. "I'd like a memory of today."

Reluctantly he moved, and she framed in the photo. "One more," she said before he could move away. "Just to make sure it's clear." But this time, she zoomed in on Van. "Got it."

When someone walking by offered to take one of the two of them, she talked him into standing with her in front of one of the wreaths. Not giving him a chance to resist, she wrapped an arm around his waist. If all she'd have of him when she left was a photo, she wanted it to be a good one.

"Why don't I make you dinner, as a thank you for helping me decorate?"

"Why don't I let you take me to Tammy's, instead?" He stepped forward and brushed his mouth over hers. "When I'm alone with you again, Gabriella, I won't be interested in food." He stepped back. "Go on and lock up the clinic. I'll wait out here."

When she came back outside, she discovered Van standing on the sidewalk, facing the clinic porch, his arms crossed over his chest.

"Oh." Despite the cold and the lightly falling snow, her heart warmed. "You made a snowman." It was small, missing a hat but he'd tied a red bandana around the neck. He'd used sticks as arms, and small rocks for the eyes and nose. And he'd placed it next to the horseshoe reindeer.

Gabriella looped her arm through his, and they walked to the diner. Along the way, they paused, studied and discussed the other storefront displays and decorations. As they walked, several people stopped them for a word or two. Some were more open with their speculative glances than others.

"Does it bother you?" Gabriella asked as they strode away from one blatant observation. "Knowing people are talking about us spending time together?"

"People always find something to talk about."

"Van." Gabriella stopped outside the diner, then shifted to face him. "If we continue, if we become more than friends, I don't want this community to think less of you after I leave."

"Gabriella, there's no if about us being 'more than friends'." He caught the end of her hair and curled it around his finger. "I'll handle whatever happens. It's better for me that you'll be leaving."

She hated the sharp jab of disappointment at hearing that he thought she'd be easy to forget.

"Hey." They both turned to see Judson grinning at them from the seat of a horse-drawn red wagon, with benches that looked like it would seat eight. "Want to take a short spin so I can check out the best route before tomorrow?"

"What do you say?" Van asked her. He didn't smile, but she saw a faint sparkle in his eyes. It was such a contrast to the intense look he'd worn moments ago.

"Are you kidding?" She grabbed his hand and headed for the wagon. "No way am I turning this down." Using Van for leverage, she stepped into the back, then snuggled beside him, their fingers entwined, beneath the wool blanket Judson handed her. "All that's missing is hot chocolate and Christmas music."

"Hot chocolate will have to wait until tomorrow. But . . ." To her delight, Judson grinned as he punched a few buttons on his phone. The joyful sounds of Jingle Bells soon filled the air. Judson kept his back to them as he guided the horses around the town square. The few people still out in the dark and cold waved, and twice they stopped to allow a truck to pass. But to Gabriella, it felt as if she and Van were alone.

"What's your favorite Christmas song? No—" she said. "Don't overthink. Just tell me what pops into your head."

"Little Drummer Boy." His shoulder rubbed her cheek when he shrugged. "I like it because it tells a story. He was a poor kid who could only give something he did with his hands. Your turn."

"Grandma Got Run Over By A Reindeer."

There was a moment of silence before he burst into a full belly laugh. It eased some of the misery that had bloomed in her heart when he'd spoken so casually about a poor kid.

"You're lying."

"It tells a story."

He drew away a little so he could look her in the eye. It took all of two seconds for her laughter to erupt.

"Damn it, Gabriella. I've going to have that stupid song in my mind all night long." He shook his head, then settled back so she could again rest her head on his shoulder. "You always make me laugh."

At that moment, no words of love could have meant more to her.

Once Judson left them at the door of the diner, Gabriella rushed inside, stomping her feet to get the blood circulating down to her freezing toes.

"Remind me to wear thick socks and boots tomorrow night."

"Well, now, this is a surprise," Tammy said, arriving at their booth seconds after they sat, the perpetual pot of coffee in her left hand. After she filled their coffee mugs, Gabriella watched as the woman patted a maternal right hand on Van's shoulder.

"Van helped me decorate the front of the clinic, so I thought I'd treat him to dinner," Gabriella said, looking around. Tinsel icicles hung from the ceiling while "Rocking Around the Christmas Tree" had replaced "Hound Dog" coming through the speakers. At each booth and table, a small evergreen, dotted with tiny red bows, sat between ceramic salt and pepper shakers shaped like Mr. and Mrs. Santa Claus.

"Your elves were busy today."

"Best day of the year. Everyone's sick of their own cooking, so they come out to eat."

"What's good today?" Gabriella asked.

"This one." Tammy nodded in Van's direction. "Used to like the beef stew."

"Sounds perfect." Van nodded his agreement.

"Did you come in here often when you first came to town?" Gabriella asked, pouring cream into her coffee.

"I worked here. It was sweeping, washing dishes, that kind of thing."

Gabriella watched him over the rim of her coffee mug. "I've done my share of that kind of work at Papa's restaurant. I also waited tables," she added when Tammy delivered their meals. "Thanks."

"I've got a slice of pie saved for you," she said to Van.

He smiled a little as she walked away. "She gave me pie with my coffee my first night in town, even though I didn't have the money to pay for it." He took a spoonful of stew. "Tammy's the one who bankrolled me when I talked about maybe staying and opening a shop here."

"Looks like you both made a good decision." She tasted the stew that was as good as advertised. She wondered if Tammy would consider giving her the recipe for her papa. Maybe if she offered his ravioli recipe in exchange.

"Was your dad disappointed you didn't want to follow in his footsteps at the restaurant?" Van asked.

"No, he knew I always wanted to be a doctor."

"A surgeon." She nodded, curious about where he was headed. He glanced around the room. "More exciting than what you've done here."

"Oh, I wouldn't say that." He looked at her, a brow lifted in question. "I've really enjoyed the variety of cases I've had here. Sure, a surgeon is often instrumental in saving lives. But I can save lives here, too. After all, I'm pretty much the sole source of medical help for miles."

"You enjoy it, being a doctor."

"I do and I believe being here has been good for me professsionally."

She shoved aside the remainder of her stew, slid one arm across the table and reached for his hand. "I'm hoping the time I have left—the time we'll share together—will be just as good for me personally."

"You know this won't go anywhere." His fingers closed tight, crushing hers. "Don't you want more?"

"Someday, yes. I want a family, children." She drew in a shallow breath at the pain that dulled his beautiful green eyes. "But until then, I want to be with you. I'm not asking for promises, Van. I'm also not making them. All I'm asking is we enjoy what we can give one another for however long we have."

"I APPRECIATE YOU coming upstairs and doing this for me."

From his perch on the stepstool, Van glanced over his shoulder. He'd been ready to leave her at the door of the apartment, not sure he could resist her, when she'd asked for his help. Now, Gabriella smiled up at him, the colored lights on her Christmas tree reflected on her face and in her brown eyes. She was barefoot, had Christmas music playing and had lit several candles.

"I didn't have much of a choice."

He turned his attention back to the tree, not sure if he was talking about helping her tonight, or ... something else. Securing the white angel she'd selected for the top, he studied his hands.

They were big, as his father's had been. He knew only too well how the pain from a fist could hurt for days. Even though it had landed him in jail, he wasn't ashamed of having used his trying to protect his mother. And he'd had little choice but to defend himself a time or two while in jail. But he'd done good with them also. He'd built a home, a business. He helped friends whenever possible. He'd made a tree topper that would, from tomorrow night on, be part of the community Christmas tradition.

He wanted his hands on Gabriella.

Any other single man he knew, and hell, even a couple of the married ones, would be thrilled with her offer of a short, no expectations affair. He should be. Neither one of them was without a past. Neither was looking for a future together.

Knowing she was using him to help fill the void of missing her family during the holidays should have made it easy for him to take her to bed. Only he had a bad feeling that once he did, it wouldn't be easy to walk away.

Stepping off the stool, he skimmed a glance over the few ornaments she'd hung, along with some white bows and ribbons.

"Stay right there," she commanded, drawing her phone out of a pocket and taking some photos.

"Give it to me." He walked her way, holding out a hand. "I'm not going to delete them," he said when she eyed him suspiciously. "Don't you want to send one to your family?" As she handed him her phone, she kissed his cheek. He wondered if he'd ever become comfortable with that easy way she had of expressing her feelings. Then he remembered he wouldn't have time to get used to it.

"How do you say Merry Christmas in Italian?" he asked, once she stood in front of the tree. He framed her in the shot, feeling his heart kick hard in his chest at how beautiful she looked. The colored lights, white bows and ribbons combined to contrast her dusky skin, dark hair and those brown eyes that looked so deeply into his.

"*Buon Natale.*"

He botched it, snapping the photo as she laughed.

"I need to go," he said, returning the phone to her.

"You don't have to."

Her soft invitation stopped him at the door. "Tonight, I do." He looked over his shoulder, then made a promise he hoped neither one of them would end up regretting.

"I'll see you tomorrow."

GABRIELLA SPENT the next morning in the clinic bursting with anticipation—and not for the next patient to arrive. She could admit being disappointed when Van left last night. But this morning, she knew he'd made the right decision to give them both time. Not that she had changed her mind.

She wanted him in her bed.

The chime of the clinic door opening popped the little fantasy she had going in her mind. Leaving her office, she frowned at the sight of Sydney leaning heavily on Ryland's arm.

"She hasn't kept anything down since yesterday," Ryland said, shifting so he could wrap a supporting arm around his wife's waist.

Gabriella went to Sydney's side, and ran a reassuring hand down her back as they walked to the exam room. She asked questions, took vitals, collected urine and blood, all while doing what she could to reassure the couple. Once she completed the basic testing, she joined her friends as they waited in her office.

"You two didn't waste much time, did you?" Sydney and Ryland looked at one another but said nothing. "Oh, come on, don't tell me you didn't suspect."

"We weren't sure," Sydney said, pressing her free hand to

her flat stomach.

"I am. Congratulations."

Gabriella's eyes filled as the couple kissed, offering a hint of the passion that had brought them to her office. Giving them a moment, she studied the notes in Sydney's file.

"Are you sure the dates you gave me are correct?"

"She's good at that kind of thing. Why?" Ryland demanded.

"A couple of her levels are elevated for this early stage of her pregnancy and you both mentioned excessive morning sickness."

"Morning, noon, and night is more like it."

"It's the reason I didn't take one of the home tests," Sydney said. "I was afraid being sick so much of the day meant something else."

"There's nothing to worry about," Gabriella said, catching the look passing between her friends. "Pregnancy sickness isn't always limited to mornings. I am going to recommend you come in for another appointment earlier than normal so we can run the tests again." She consulted her calendar, then suggested a date and time. At that moment, she realized, that while she would get the test results back, she wouldn't be in town long enough to watch her friend blossom with the pregnancy. Keeping her professional face in place, she rose from behind her desk and approached.

"I'm not worried," she repeated, reaching for Sydney's hands to squeeze in reassurance. "So you shouldn't be either." She rattled off a few suggestions for helping to ease the sickness. "If you want, I can prescribe some medication." Sydney shook her head. "Okay then. Go home. No work," she instructed, then smiled, leaned forward and kissed both of Sydney's cheeks. "Call your family and friends with the good news."

She walked the couple to the front door, watching as they stepped off the porch, then stopped and turned to one another.

Standing there, focused on each other and ignoring someone calling out a greeting, Gabriella was stunned by the burn of tears climbing up her throat. Watching them, she couldn't stop the comparison of her temporary status and intention to be with

Van, with Sydney's original plan to stay for a short two weeks while she helped Ryland secure funding for his ranch.

Her friends had found love, and had made a commitment to one another. They, and the ranch they now managed together, were integral parts of this community. And in a few months, they would become a family.

She and Van had formed a friendship and were on the cusp of becoming intimate. But, by mutual agreement, that was as far as their relationship would extend. In less than a month, they'd go their separate ways.

And she also realized she'd leave more than Van when she returned to Chicago. All the friendships she'd made here would continue—sharing the joys and heartaches, the holidays, the ups and downs of their relationships—as they had before she came to town. She returned inside, her eye traveling to the horseshoe Christmas tree Van had made. Even that would be left behind.

She jumped when the clinic door opened. Two men, both in jackets and hats covered in snow entered. One clutched his hand, which was wrapped tight in a blue bandana.

"Doc," greeted the other man. "Jim here damn near cut his finger off with a saw."

"I barely nicked it," Jim argued.

Grateful for the diversion from her thoughts, Gabriella crossed the room. Lifting the bandana growing dark with blood, she saw Jim had almost been right. "It's more than a nick, but it's not so deep that I can't stitch you up here."

Later, after the two men left and she cleaned up the exam room, she thought of what she'd be doing in a little over a month. Surgery would become her main focus. And she had to admit, she'd miss all the little moments of general practice—the joy of telling a young couple they were expecting, the personal touch of having time to spend talking with an elderly patient who wanted attention more than she needed care. She wouldn't be entertained by two friends teasing each other as a distraction while she performed minor surgery.

Did that mean she'd found more satisfaction practicing general medicine?

"No," she insisted, walking out of the exam room and heading for the office. "It's just that's all I've known for these months." Surely once she returned to Chicago and began her fellowship, she'd rediscover her passion for surgery.

Picking up the phone, she called her grandfather. A short call later, she'd been reassured he expected to hear any day of her acceptance into the fellowship program. As usual, she had to once again defend her choice of pediatric surgery rather than follow his footsteps into cardiology.

Feeling steadier and more in control, she closed the clinic and went upstairs to prepare for tonight.

Chapter Six

HER BREATH PUFFED out like a snowy cloud in the cold as she scanned the crowd, looked for Van among the people roaming the streets. Since she spotted quite a few faces she didn't recognize, she assumed the mayor's outreach advertising had hit the mark.

While most of the activities were planned for tonight, several booths were already open and busy. At Unique Finds, a recently opened shop showcasing local artists and craftspeople, she purchased some beautiful hand-painted Christmas cards. She did some other shopping, both for Christmas gifts and for herself. In fact, she bought so much, that she had to return to the apartment twice rather than drag packages around all day. Children darted from the games arena over to where various animals endured, for the most part, the petting of eager little hands. She stood well out of the line of fire as one group of teenagers, hiding in an alley between stores, laughingly ambushed another passing group of other teens with the snowballs they'd packed. It was such an innocent event, one far removed from the inner-city image of gangs and drive-by shootings. After the snowball fight ended, both groups headed for a food booth to refuel the unending appetite of youth.

She grinned for a photo as she sat on the lap of the aptly named high school teacher Van had told her about, who completed his outfit with an honest-to-God fluffy white beard and red suit.

She took photos of her own, sent them in texts to her family who had followed tradition and had gathered at her papa's restaurant after a day of work or decorating, and sniffed back tears at the replies filled with regret or teasing about her being so far away. She pitched in to help the volunteers, delivering supplies where needed, taking over supervision of the children coloring printed pictures of Santa, Christmas trees, or reindeer while someone took a break. She served eagerly accepted coffee to other volunteers. The festive mood boosted her holiday spirit, and greetings and shared conversations heightened her sense of belonging.

She knew the instant Van spotted her. A sudden burst of heat erupted in her belly, fired its way up her throat, making her unbearably thirsty. Her heart hammered with anticipation. Still, she was calm when she turned around and met his gaze.

He stood a head above other people in the crowd. Today he again wore a cowboy hat and a thick coat against the winter cold, though his hands were bare. She knew there was something in his past he wasn't ready to share with her, and while she couldn't say the past didn't matter, she knew that the man he was today—with his sense of honor, his gentleness, and his work ethic—appealed to her in a way no man ever had before. Assured that she was making the right decision to be with him, she walked over and took his cold hand in hers.

"I've been waiting for you."

He studied her for a long moment. Around them, sounds became muted, and crowds passed by like shadows. The light softened as the sun lowered.

"Why don't I buy you some hot chocolate?" he finally said.

"Why don't you?"

All the community atmosphere that had given her so much pleasure throughout the day faded into the background. She no longer wished her family was here to share this time. Neither she nor Van sought out the company of anyone else. They circulated in and out of the crowd, unaware of the activities going on around them, solely focused on one another. He told her of the work he'd done that day, she told him about stitching a finger. When he winced, she teased him about being so afraid of a tiny needle. He countered that no matter the size, needles jabbed a hole in you. They shared a bag of roasted chestnuts while snuggled under a blanket in the back of Judson's wagon, this time with others along for the ride. But they may as well have been as alone as they'd been that first time. She couldn't recall ever being so engrossed in another person, or experiencing the giddy joy of knowing that person felt the same.

Their bubble of privacy was finally pierced by the mayor's announcement over the loud speaker that the tree lighting was about to begin.

"I'll be waiting for you," Gabriella whispered, kissing him.

Wanting to extend this sensation that she and Van were alone, she avoided friends, choosing instead to stand alone. Only during that brief isolation, she was suddenly blindsided by the realization that this time next year, she'd be back in Chicago.

From a stage to the left of the large tree, there were the obligatory words of greeting, as well as recognition for the organizers and volunteers who'd put the night together. Announcements were made for the schedule, not only for the remainder of the night, but the entire holiday season, including mention of the carnival held in the elementary school along with the special candlelit ceremony early on Christmas Eve.

"And now," Mayor Scott said, lifting a box from the back of the stage, "I want to thank Donovan Ferguson for making the topper for our community tree." She paused as applause erupted. "When he agreed, I knew he'd make us something memorable. But I didn't expect something so meaningful." Gabriella felt the first prick of tears as she watched Van shift uneasily on his feet. "Christmas is the season of lights, and lighting this tree is the reason we're here tonight." She smiled. "But we're also here because we're friends, neighbors, family." She drew out the circular form from the box and held it up.

Before she could continue, Van stepped forward. Obviously surprised, the mayor looked at him for a moment before passing the topper to him.

"I, uh . . ." He cleared his throat. "I was flattered when the mayor asked me to make this." He lifted the topper a little. "I didn't know if it was the best idea." He paused, his lips slanting ever so slightly with humor before his gaze took on a dark intensity. "But Burton Springs has become home, an unexpected one. You could say it's been the brightest light in my life." His gaze traveled the crowd, locked with Gabriella's. "So I made a ring of metal candles with varying heights of flame. In between the candles are hands and hearts, representing the friendships we all share." He cleared his throat. "This is my way of thanking everyone who's ever made me feel welcome."

As if he'd suddenly run out of words, he shoved the topper into the mayor's hands and stepped back. Cheers and applause broke out through the crowd, and Gabriella let out a sigh.

The mayor granted the crowd ten minutes to get a close-up look of the piece before it was lifted to the top of tree. When Van tried to slide away, she snagged his arm and had him posing for a photo. Of course, people then clustered around Van.

Pride filled Gabriella, making it easy for her to stand aside, not distracting any of the attention Van deserved. Bit by bit, she saw his shoulders relax, heard him laugh at some comment, nod and shake hands at the end of a conversation. He was more than part of this community—he had more than friends here. He had an extended family—the family she suspected he'd never had before settling in Burton Springs. People here had been as welcoming to her, even knowing her position was only temporary.

As the town gathered around the base of the tree, the topper was put into place and the lights switched on. The children's choir began singing Silent Night, and soon everyone joined in.

Her patience drained away. The reminder that she wouldn't be here next year drove home the realization of just how little time she and Van had together. She'd shared him enough for tonight. Now it was time for her to be selfish, to reach for and give the intimacy she craved.

Pushing through the crowd, she reached for his hand. "Van," she said, leaning forward to whisper in his ear. "Will you come home with me?"

While he stared at her, his eyes narrowed, she questioned if she'd read him wrong. She could see the hesitation, the questions and concerns.

"We both have reasons for being careful," she said, offering as much as accepting. "And we both have reasons for not believing in promises. But we also know how long and lonely the nights can be." She lifted a hand to his chest, felt the steady drum of his heart. "We know we can be with one another, enjoy one another, without expectation."

"I don't think so."

Disappointment was a hot streak trailing from her throat to the pit of her stomach. His rejection slashed at her pride. Then he moved closer and cupped her face in his hands.

"I'm not going to be careful. At least not the entire night." His rare smile, stunningly sexy, had another kind of fire pooling between her thighs. "But I will make you one promise, one you can count on." He leaned forward and whispered a suggestion that had her moaning as she closed her eyes.

"It is going to be a long night, Gabriella." He lifted his head and stared at her with his beautiful green eyes, thrilling her with the sensual look that mirrored the words he'd whispered. "But it's not going to be lonely."

They all but ran through the crowd, ignoring calls, side-stepping people who got in their way. Then they tore up the apartment stairs, shedding coats as they went. Gabriella had never before known the kind of urgency that rushed through her now. Just inside the door to the apartment, she turned to him and lifted her hands to his shirt. Her hands trembled with the effort it took to unbutton it rather than rip it off.

"*Ti sbrighi.* Hurry," she said, kissing his face, moaning as his hands roamed over her, stoking the fire inside her. When his hands cupped her breasts, her head fell back. His teeth and lips nipped at her throat, lowered to capture a nipple through her dress, generating needle stabs of pleasure with each pull of his mouth. "Here," she begged, sliding a hand down his bare chest, slipping into the waistband of his jeans, flicking open the button. "Now."

"No."

He caught her hand before she could wrap it around him. He swept her into his arms and carried her over to her bed. "Here," he said, lowering her to the mattress. His hands, rough from his work, excited her even more as he stripped her clothes.

She had no defense against this man. And she didn't want one. Pressure built inside her, the most erotic pressure, as he tormented her with touches that robbed her of thought, and his mouth devoured hers. Her skin grew damp, her breathing labored as the hunger between them grew stronger, bolder.

There was urgency . . . and a staggering need. But beneath it all, there was something else—something that veered a little too closely to tenderness. Gabriella shoved it aside and grabbed hold of the searing heat, hoping it would burn away everything but the incredible need blazing between them.

It took little more than a skim of his fingertip over her center to have her hips arching, wanting yet more, as her body exploded.

"Van. Now. Please," she begged.

"Wait." He pressed his forehead to hers, drew in a deep breath. "I need to get a condom."

"I'm on birth control." Her hands cupped his face, lifted it so their eyes held. "I haven't been with anyone for more than seven months."

"I'm healthy. I promise."

"I trust you, Van." She kissed him. "I want you." Her hands reached for his, fingers curling tight, when he rose over her. He stared deep into her eyes and plunged into her.

And like everything else between them tonight, their climaxes came hard, fast, and together.

"No, don't," she said, her voice thick with satisfaction when Van started to move away. Her eyes were closed but her lips curved. "It took me long enough to get you into my bed. I'm in no hurry for you to leave it."

"I did promise you a long night." Before she could suspect, he rolled, bringing her with him, until he lay on his back and she straddled his hips.

With an abandon she'd never known, her hands scooped back her hair as she arched her back, giving him greater access to use his fingers to find and arouse the center of her. Her hips began to rock as she rode him with a slow and steady rhythm that gave them the luxury to softly give and take what they'd skimmed over in that first rush of need and desire.

LATER, AFTER THEY managed to tease and refresh in a shower barely large enough for both of them, Van slid on his jeans and went in search of his shirt. He discovered Gabriella standing at the short kitchen counter, making something. Off to one side, he saw a half-filled glass of wine, another glass of sparkling water. She wore a short robe and had pulled her hair back into a low ponytail. She'd lit the candles she had scattered throughout the room and had turned on Christmas music. Beneath the Christmas tree she'd trimmed with multi-colored lights, shopping bags waited for wrapping.

These were the small details that made a difference, the kind of thoughtful gestures that were a natural and intrinsic part of her. The kind of small touches that made a woman more than a lover.

He'd had more than his share of one-night stands before, had been with women who knew nothing, and cared less, about his past. He'd known all they wanted was what he could give them in bed. Afterward, it had been easy to walk away, to believe he had no interest in anything more.

Gabriella wouldn't be easy to forget. He liked her, way more than was wise. And if he wasn't careful, that liking could turn into something he'd long ago given up on believing he could have in his life.

Crossing the room, he slid his arms around her waist, closing his eyes against the tug at his heart when she leaned back against him. "What are you doing?"

"Grating some cheese. I thought I'd scramble us some eggs."

"Don't you just open a package from the store?"

She shifted so she could give him a mock-stern look over her shoulder. "No, I do not."

"Gabriella." He turned her to face him, cupped her cheeks in his hands. Her eyes went dark, not with desire this time but with worry. "What are you doing, here, with me?"

She leaned forward to lightly brush his lips with hers. "I'm enjoying being with a man who gives me something no one ever has. Acceptance," she said before he could ask. "All my life, I've tried to be what everyone wanted, what they expected of me. The dutiful daughter, the annoying sister." She shrugged. "When my parents and grandfather realized I wanted to go into medicine, they expected me to succeed. *I* expected me to succeed." Her eyes darkened. "When I was with Timothy, he expected me to remain in the shadows."

Van brushed at her cheek.

"Even when I came here, people thought I'd be like Doctor Leonard, to treat them the way he always had. You, on the other hand, have asked for nothing but what I'm willing to give. And even then, you tried to stop tonight from happening. So I had no choice but to make it impossible for you to turn away. And desperate times called for desperate measures." Her eyes grew bright with amusement, and she pressed her mouth to his for a long, long kiss. "I love medicine. I want to be a good doctor. But you see *me*, Van. You give me the chance to be more than a doctor. To just be a woman."

"There's nothing just about you."

"See?" He stepped back when tears filled her eyes. "No wonder I want to be with you."

"Gabriella, tonight meant something to me. I don't want you to think otherwise."

"I don't." Closing her eyes, she drew him close again, holding him tight. Almost as if she didn't want to let him go. "Tonight there is no past. No future. There's just us."

She kissed his cheek, then turned back to the counter. "Why don't you make toast while I scramble the eggs?"

Trying to lighten the mood, he made a show of looking around the small kitchen space. "What? You mean you want me to use store bought bread?"

"*Sapientone.*"

And because she laughed when she said it, he didn't care what she called him. When she plated the eggs and toast, they decided to sit on the floor beside the Christmas tree rather than at the table.

"I should get a train," she said. "Like the one Carter and Audra have under their tree."

He looked around, nudged a shopping bag with his foot. "You don't have much room in here."

"There is always room for Christmas."

He took a forkful of egg. "My mom almost always burned eggs when she cooked them." He kept his gaze on his plate, but he was aware that Gabriella had stilled and stared at him. "Otherwise, she cooked pretty good." His smile came a little easier. "Mostly stuff from a box," he said, and though it sounded stiff, she laughed. "She cooked best when the old man wasn't home. She relaxed then. Anyway . . ." He shrugged, scooped up a forkful of eggs. "This is better."

"You have such a great kitchen." Gabriella paused, cleared her throat. "Do you enjoy cooking?"

"Not as much as eating." Her laughter was a little easier this time. "Mostly, Audra told me how I should build it."

"You have good friends."

"I do. You know what you said earlier? About how I see you differently than everyone does?" She met his gaze, her eyes dark as she nodded. "No one's ever given me time the way you do."

She set her plate aside, did the same with his. Then she moved so she could straddle him. "Let's give each other some of that time now."

WINCING A LITTLE, Gabriella rolled over and pressed her nose into the empty pillow. The bed was considerably softer than the floor—and the equally hard contours of Van's body— had been last night. Not that she regretted a single second or ache. She drew in a breath, caught the faint odor of heated iron she would forever associate with Van.

He'd kissed her awake two hours earlier to say good-bye. She smiled. He hadn't gone home as early as he'd planned.

She'd wanted this affair with him, believing she'd be able to leave Burton Springs, and Van, with little more than fond memories. Only the more she learned about him, the more she got to know and understand him, she feared leaving wouldn't be so easy.

But today was Sunday, and she had no appointments . . . which gave her way too much time to think. So she got busy. After an indulgent shower, she took care of some chores before wrapping the gifts she'd bought the day before. Since she'd always believed a Christmas tree looked empty without them, she put the brightly wrapped presents under the tree. Van had been right, she admitted. She had no room under the tree for a train.

Maybe, if her luck held and there were no emergencies, she'd drive out to see him, and even cook dinner for him in his spacious kitchen. With that in mind, she headed out to go to the store.

Deciding she could walk, she strolled past storefronts, recall-ing how many had watched her and Van decorate the clinic. She passed workers straightening lamppost wreaths knocked off-kilter from last night's crowd, then paused, watching as a couple posed for a photo in front of the huge Christmas tree topped by Van's design, while a mother and father admonished their toddler for climbing onto the replica of Santa's sleigh.

People nodded greetings or passed by as they rushed from warm interiors to their vehicles or other shops. She didn't mind. The air was cold, but there was no wind. She waved at Kendall Montgomery when she drove by in her Sheriff's car, suddenly wondering what it would be like to take a life rather than save one. But she didn't want to think of medicine, and the looming last days of her stay here. She wanted nothing more than to enjoy the atmosphere of the postcard-perfect image of Christmas in a small town.

Perhaps her mood, or some need inside her was what brought her to the simple white church. She knew the red doors were there all year and not just for the holiday. But both doors were hung with lovely wreaths wrapped in white ribbon and balls.

"Excuse me," a breathless woman said as she ran after the child racing up the steps. When she pulled open the right door, music flooded out. Music and voices.

Drawn, Gabriella followed.

She blinked to make the adjustment from bright outside light to the more subdued ambiance of the church interior. She watched the child fling her coat onto a pew without pause as she hurried to wedge between two other girls on the bottom row of the choir. With barely an indrawn breath, she joined the song, "Oh Come All Ye Faithful".

Other parents were clustered in the first few pews, but Gabriella walked in and sat in one of the back ones. She smelled candles, the pine of the tree in a corner decorated with white and silver ornaments, and let the music, the innocence of the children's voices, pour over her.

They were practicing for the Christmas Eve program. As the town had done for the night of the tree lighting, they would gather for songs and fellowship before going home and tucking these children into their beds. Before parents, probably exhausted from all the work of the holiday, arranged packages and surprises from Santa.

Would she and Van spend that night together? One of the last nights they'd have before she returned to Chicago?

The children's voices echoed in her head as she walked out and answered her vibrating phone. "This is Dr. Santini."

"Where are you?" Rhonda asked.

"I was taking a walk. Is something wrong?"

"You mean other than you're crazy enough to be walking around outside in this cold? I thought maybe you weren't answering the door because you were still burning up the sheets with Van."

"You're at the clinic?"

"The door to your apartment. Kathy Davis and I are driving out to Evergreen to help Ellen, and Sydney if she's feeling up to it, decorate the cabins and cookhouse. Audra said she would try to stop by. Want to come along?"

"Sydney told you her news?"

"Are you kidding? I think she told everyone in town last night."

"I'd love to help out."

"Where are you? We'll pick you up."

"No, go on ahead. I should have my car in case I get an emergency call."

"Really? You think I'd fall for that line? Never mind," she said before Gabriella could comment. "I'm just happy to hear Van finally made his move."

"Trust me, he's got great moves."

The silence on the other end of the phone was very satisfying. It pleased her to know her friends knew about her and Van, and they obviously approved. It was so different from the secrecy she'd been compelled to keep about her and Timothy.

"I'll see you soon."

SHE TOOK SOME time to run up to the apartment and pack up a few things before driving to Evergreen. Once there, she managed to evade or ignore comments and questions as the women hung wreaths, garland, and decorated the tree in the cookhouse. They shared wine, laughter and the tasty desserts and appetizers provided by Ellen. Gabriella was pleased that Sydney had more color on her cheeks, although she still showed signs of early-pregnancy fatigue.

And later, after deciding to enjoy every moment possible, she drove out to Van's place. When he opened the door, she said, "I wasn't sure . . ." Her words died, and the bags in her hands fell to the floor when he reached for her and pulled her inside. Pushing her against the wall, he devoured her mouth.

"All day," he said, making quick work of her coat buttons. "I thought of you. Wanted you." She groaned with pleasure when his hands closed on her breasts.

The man definitely had some great moves.

Chapter Seven

MONDAY MORNING, Gabriella followed Van's example and rose early. While he shaved, she made the bed before heading into the kitchen.

"I don't expect you to cook every time we're together," Van said, joining her.

"I love your kitchen. And I like to feed you."

He poured coffee, then leaned back against the counter, looking more relaxed than she could recall ever seeing him. "Trust me, if this keeps up, I'll need to go on a diet."

She leaned over to kiss his cheek. "As your physician and your lover, I can attest you don't have an ounce of fat on you." She frowned, then looked up from where she sliced bananas. "Wait. There was no patient file on you in the clinic until I started one to note the injury to your hand. Why not?"

"I'm never sick."

"Van, you should still have regular checkups."

"Never have." He shrugged. "I'm fine."

"Sure, you are now. But the whole purpose of regular checkups is to get ahead of any potential problems. You could have high blood pressure, or something in your family history . . ."

"I'm fine."

Mention of his family put that hard tone in his voice. She accepted it even if she didn't understand the cause for it. But more than her medical integrity pushed her to try. She set down the knife, wiping her hands on a towel before she gripped his arm. "Please, Van. Come into the clinic for a basic checkup. As a favor to me?"

"I did you a favor yesterday."

Suddenly cold, she stepped back. "I see."

"No." He slammed down his mug, then reached for her hand, swearing when she evaded his reach. "I don't mean sex." He scrubbed hands down his face. "Wait here." He stared at her. "Please." After a brief hesitation, she nodded. "It's in the workshop. I'll be right back."

While he was gone, she rubbed at the throbbing ache between her breasts. Hating the urge to scoop up her things and leave, she made herself stand and wait. Finally, he came back inside, his cheeks flushed.

"I made this yesterday. While I thought of you."

She glanced down at what he offered. And had to blink away sudden tears.

"It's not a train," he said needlessly. "But that's beyond my ability anyway." She shook her head, still staring at what he held. "Plus you really don't have room under your tree for a train. But this?" He took her hand, placing the iron replica of a simple wagon design in her palm. "Well, it's something I thought of. Since, you know, we took the ride and all."

"Van." Her fingers closed tight as she stepped forward and buried her face in his neck. "It's wonderful. Thank you."

"It's small enough that you can pack it your suitcase when you leave."

"I'll put it under my tree every Christmas." She lifted her head, kissed him. "And I'll think of you."

Stepping back, she tilted her head. "You know, if you came into the clinic for a checkup today, and then stayed with me tonight, you'd see how it looks under the tree. Since you don't have one yourself."

He gave her one of his rare, quick grins that never failed to charm her. "Walked straight into that one, didn't I? Okay."

"I promise to be gentle."

"I hope not." He pulled her in for a hot kiss. "Just how big are those exam tables?"

"Not big, but they are softer than the floor."
"Why don't we plan on making it to your bed?"

"I'll put you down in my appointment book."

After breakfast and a warm kiss good-bye, Gabriella drove

back to town. Upstairs in the apartment, she placed Van's wagon front and center under the tree, then just stared at it for a few minutes before heading down to the clinic. In anticipation of his appointment, she called up his skimpy patient file on her computer, and noted the tests she wanted to run.

Later that day, she was smiling as she walked one of her patients back to the reception area. Ever since she'd first arrived in Burton Springs, she'd been trying to convince Franklin James to come in for a physical. The patient file she'd inherited listed his age as eighty-eight, but he insisted he was five years younger. No one, and certainly not the vitals she'd just noted in his file, would argue. Today, he hadn't made an appointment, but had just suddenly appeared.

"Franklin, I'm so glad you came by." She'd also talked him into getting a flu shot.

"Been telling you there's nothing wrong with me."

"And we want to keep it that way."

"I've heard good things about you. It's a damn shame you're going to be leaving."

Absurdly touched, she remained silent as the door to the clinic opened, and a man, not much more than a boy, she didn't recognize entered. "I'll be right with you," she told him, and returned her attention to Mr. James. "I'll send you a report once I get the blood test results back." She grinned. "But I don't think there'll be anything to say other than you're in excellent health."

"Keeping busy's the trick." He glanced over her shoulder, leaned down a little. "You want me to stay a little longer?"

"I'll be fine." Flattered, she rose on her toes and kissed his cheek—something she could never get away with in a big hospital or a busy practice. "You have a Merry Christmas." When the door closed behind him, she turned to the new arrival.

Then froze when she saw the knife he held by his side.

Sadly, it wasn't the first time she'd faced potential danger. It was however, the first time she'd done so without the cushion of a busy hospital, staff and security close at hand.

"I need some medicine," he growled.

"I don't keep drugs here."

"Don't give me that. You're a doctor. I know you've got something." He waved the blade with an erratic gesture that had her blood turning to ice. "All I want's some pills. Give them to me and I won't hurt you."

She nodded and extended a hand. "This way."

She made sure not to walk too close, her gaze searching the room for anything she could use as a weapon. At the door to what they used as a lab, she saw the tray of blood vials she'd taken from Mr. James. Reaching into her lab coat pocket for the keys, she moved to the locked wall cabinet. She felt the man's breath on her neck as she shifted the keys to her left hand.

Before he could ask, demand or question, she grabbed the needle she'd neglected to dispose of, swung around and jabbed it into his neck as her right elbow slammed into his throat. She felt a nick, heard his howl of rage as she shoved while swiping the keys she'd slipped between her fingers down his cheek. He staggered back, giving her just enough room to run out, slamming the door closed behind her.

He chased after her as she ran into the reception area. At the last second, she changed course, but it wasn't enough. As he grabbed her hair, her hand closed around one of the iron ornaments Van had made for the horseshoe Christmas tree. With the momentum of the man behind her pulling, coupled with her fear and adrenaline, she managed to snap the star free of the top horseshoe, then swung around and shoved the point of the star deep into his temple. Refusing to think, she struck again, then again before he stumbled back, his eyes rolling as he dropped to the floor. Her breath heaving, she stomped her foot on his wrist and fumbled in the pocket of her lab coat for her phone. She swung around when the clinic door opened, and the star and phone fell from her suddenly lax fingers.

"Van."

He rushed to her, gathering her in his arms. "Are you hurt?"

"No." She sucked in a breath. "I should treat his wounds," she murmured against his shoulder.

"Are you out of your mind?"

She took a deep breath, stepped back. "I'm a doctor, Van. I

can't just let him lie there. He's bleeding."

"So are you."

She looked down at the thin ribbon of blood on her arm. "It's just a scratch." Laughter bubbled up, hysteria on the verge of escaping. "Let me tend my patient, then I'll take care of this."

Van shoved away, swearing under his breath, his eyes dark. With alarm, she watched him reach down, grab the man's shirt and lift him to his feet, emphasizing the size and strength differences between the two men. His other hand opened and closed into a fist, making the tendons on his forearm pop.

Unable to protest or look away, she watched as Van trembled with the strain of holding back the violence he so wanted to release. Her heart gave way a little with the realization he both wanted to avenge her and yet he accepted there was nothing else for him to do.

"Call the police, Gabriella. Then you can treat him."

She went for supplies, returning as Kendall Montgomery rushed in, gun drawn. "I'm treating his wound," Gabriella said.

"Wait." Kendall secured her gun, then moved to where Van continued to hold the man still, and cuffed his hands behind his back.

When another officer arrived, Kendall took Van to one side, taking notes on a small pad as they talked. After the other officer left with the suspect, Gabriella gave Kendall her side of what happened.

"We'll need to close the clinic while we take pictures and gather evidence." Kendall smiled in apology. "Your Christmas tree is going to be without a star for a while."

"I'll make you another one," Van said from where he stood watching her. His usual calm steadiness had returned. His eyes looked haunted and miserable.

"You might need to work on your welding skills. It came off pretty easy."

"Listen," Kendall said, crouching in front of her, gripping her hand. "I know what it's like to go through something like this. Do you want to come out to our house for the night?"

"She's coming home with me."

"No." Gabriella stood and although she would privately admit her legs were shaky, she kept her balance as she walked to him. "I can't leave. Please understand. If I walk away, if I run scared, no one in this town will ever trust me as their doctor."

When he remained silent, she looked at Kendall. "I trust you'll lock up when you're done?" At the nod, she turned back to Van. "Looks like your checkup will have to wait until another day."

The anger in his gaze evaporated. "Gabriella."

She shook her head. She couldn't break down here. "I really want a long, hot shower, followed by a glass of wine. Will you come with me?"

Holding his hand, she led him to the door leading to the interior set of stairs. Once in the apartment, she began to tremble. Without a word, Van wrapped her in his arms.

The tears she'd been holding back flooded free. He didn't say a word, just simply held her, stroking a strong, sure hand up and down her back. When she shed the last tear and gulped in a deep breath, he lifted her face.

"No, don't." She kept her eyes closed. "I'm a mess."

"You're beautiful. I've always thought you beautiful." His lips were gentle enough to have more tears threaten. "Go, take your shower. You'll feel better." He kissed her again. "I'll be here when you get out."

The shower did wonders for her morale, and for the few aches she hadn't noticed before. Deciding there was no reason to bother with makeup, she stepped around the privacy screen. Her heart immediately rose into her throat.

He sat at the table where he'd set out dishes, two of them, and had lit a candle to compliment the lights on her Christmas tree. A single glass of wine had already been poured.

"Well, this helps boost my mood even more than the shower."

He rose and pulled out her chair for her. With a lifted brow, she sat, shivering a little when he pressed a light kiss to the side of her neck. She watched as he bent at the waist to take her leftover lasagna out of the oven. He did have one fine butt.

"I would say you didn't have to go to all this trouble, but there are few things sexier than a man making dinner."

"You made it."

She smiled as she lifted her glass, and took a swallow. "True," she agreed as he returned to the table. "But you heated it up." She waited until he sat back down before she closed a hand over his. "Thank you."

"This is better than anything you'd get at my place. I guess you were right to not want to go there."

"It had nothing to not wanting to go to your house. I love your house. I know you disagree with me being here tonight, so thank you, Van, for staying with me." She sipped her wine. "Why don't I come to your place tomorrow? We can bake Christmas cookies."

"How can you be so calm?" he demanded, dropping his fork on the plate. The chink of metal hitting the glass echoed in the room.

"I'm not, you know I'm not. Van, you held me when I fell apart." Unsure where this was leading, she set down her own fork but didn't reach for his hand. He didn't look at her, his breathing was increasingly jerky, and she didn't care for the pallor of his skin. If she didn't know better, she'd swear he was the one reliving the bad experience.

"When I walked in . . ." He scraped a hand over his mouth. "And saw that guy on the floor, all the blood . . . you. I wanted to pound him into the floor."

"I know."

He spread his hands wide. "I have big hands. Like my father. I've always been afraid that if I let my temper go, I'd use them the way he did."

"Oh, Van." She reached for him, trying not to be hurt when he avoided her. "You could never be like that."

He slammed the chair back, then rose and started to pace the tiny space. Then, as if her distress had reached out to stroke a calm hand over him, he stopped, closed his eyes and drew in a breath. When he opened his eyes again, she saw a tremor of uncertainty in them.

"I could never help my mother."

Oh, Van. I'm sorry. I'm so sorry.

He shot one glance at her wine, then looked away. "I told you my father drank. He drank when he was happy, when he was hurt, when he was angry." He sucked in a breath, much the way a diver did before heading down into the ocean depths.

"He hit my mother the same way. The one time he tried to go after me—I think I was seven or eight—she stepped in."

"She protected you," Gabriella whispered.

He laughed and shook his head. "No, that would make sense. No, Gabriella, she waited 'til good old Dad passed out and then she took the strap to me."

She rose to her feet. "She whipped you?"

"She told me to never again interfere with what went on between her and my father. I should have listened to her, should have known she'd never take my side. So for a while I did what she asked and never got in between them."

Seeing her today, bruised, angry, and defiant against his protective offer to take her to his place, where he believed he could protect her, must have brought it all back. How long had he suffered and felt guilty for failing to shield his mother, she wondered, watching him move back to sit at the table. She lowered to her chair, wanting, needing to reach out, even though she knew this wasn't the time.

"When I was sixteen," he continued, "I got it in my mind that I'd grown enough to take him on, to make sure he stopped pounding on her." He glanced at Gabriella. "He'd started taking swings at my little sister. Just pops on the butt, telling her to move out of his way. But I didn't trust him, didn't think it would stay with little pops for long. So Friday night—payday, which always meant a stop off at a local bar on the way home—he came home, ripped and yelling at anyone who crossed his path." She trembled, just like the hand he lifted to take a long drink from his water glass.

"Before he started in on my mother, I stepped in front of him. He laughed, said mean things. I think, I really think, he was baiting me, hoping I'd do something that would give him an excuse to take a swing at me. When I didn't, and God alone knows why I didn't, he got meaner. It might have been a stand-off, if my mother had kept her distance. But she didn't. She took a step forward and he turned on her. The next instant, she was crying out and falling to the floor. Like a red flag, it set me off. I started pounding on him." His breath heaved in and out in quick bursts.

"We crashed around the room, like two dogs in a cage. I heard screams, crying. Then, nothing." His brief silence was worse than the images he gave her. "I woke to find the cops lifting me off the floor, cuffing my hands. My mother was screaming, saying that I'd attacked my father, that the whole incident was my fault. I'm the one who'd put the bruise on her face." He laughed, a harsh sound. "And my father? He claimed he'd been trying to keep me from going after her. So the cops hauled me off to jail."

Gabriella was so stunned she could only stare. He continued to look anywhere but at her.

"My sister had been at a friend's house—she was hardly more than a kid—so they didn't ask her about any previous beat-ings. They wouldn't have listened to her, anyway."

But you were only a kid too, Gabriella wanted to say.

"I took my public defender's advice, pleaded guilty and was sentenced to eighteen months in juvey. That's where I picked up the blacksmith stuff." He shrugged. "It was a way to keep busy, to stay away from the gangs and out of fights."

He spoke so calmly, so matter-of-factly about gangs and fights. Not for a second did she believe he'd escaped as easily as he claimed.

"About three months into my time, I found out the old man had tried to rape my sister. She was fourteen." Gabriella sucked in a sharp breath. "From what I've pieced together, my mom came in and found him. She ripped into him, grabbing a lamp and smashing it on his head. Then she and my sister went to the police." Gabriella admired him even more for so calmly accepting his mother's protective behavior toward his sister when she'd been the one responsible for him being in jail.

"The old man was only in jail about four weeks when someone shivved him, leaving him to bleed out in the shower." Van shook his head. "As mean as some of those guys in jail can be, they don't stomach anyone who messes with kids."

"Your mother? Sister?" Gabriella asked.

"I looked them up when I got out of jail. Mom had a job, and Rosie was getting ready to leave for college on a scholarship." He shrugged, avoiding her gaze. "They didn't need me so I set out. Ended up here."

"You think telling me this will change my mind about you. You honestly believe I'll think less of you for hearing you spent time, time you didn't deserve, in juvenile detention."

She slid off the chair and knelt at his knees. "You know what I think, what I see, when I look at you? I see a man who had a rotten childhood, made all the worse by trying to do the right thing." She shook her head, stopping him from interrupting. "Even so, he took that bad turn in his life and made something of himself, he built a business, a home, became a valuable member of the town. Did he make mistakes along the way? Sure. Who doesn't?" She gripped his hands.

"Your past influenced you. But today, you proved you're a good man. One who can call on control when it's needed. You didn't protect me today, Van, but you were here, you *are* here, when I asked you to be."

She stood, pulled him up. "Come with me," she whispered, walking backward toward the bed. "Be with me."

"Gabriella, no. You've been through enough today."

"I need you, Van. Let me show you."

Combining light kisses with gentle touches, she stripped him, then removed her clothes. Her heart broke at the cautious look in his eyes.

She stroked hands over him, hoping to soothe along with seduce. Her mouth moved in a leisurely exploration, offering pleasure. For both of them.

She wanted to give him all the tenderness he'd never known.

When he reached for her, she almost shied away, wanting only to give and not take. But too many people had turned from him. So she let him do what he wanted.

The big hands he feared could harm instead enticed, excited. His clever fingers urged her up and over the first peak. His eyes now glowed with desire rather than misery.

With a slow, welcoming slide she took him in, leaning down to feast on his mouth.

Together they surrendered to the moment.

After, as they lay quiet, wrapped in each other's arms, Gabriella stroked his chest. "Van." She rose on an elbow and looked down at him, smiling at the satisfied glaze in his eyes. She hated to erase it, but felt certain she was about to.

"You should contact your mother and sister. Let them know you're okay." She covered his mouth with her hand. "How can you forgive yourself, if you're still wondering whether or not they have. Think about it." She replaced her hand with her lips, and settled down in the crook of his arm. *"Buona Notte."*

WITH A SLOW movement he hadn't depended on since he'd been an apprentice, Van folded and hammered the softened iron into the curve of the scrollwork initial that would be the centerpiece of a door. He needed to concentrate, to pay attention to the work. In spite of his efforts, thoughts of Gabriella, and the way he'd spilled his guts to her, continued to intrude.

At least he'd kept his mouth shut, and hadn't told her that he'd fallen in love with her.

He'd known how he felt about her before last night. But, hell, the way she'd accepted, simply accepted, the news of his childhood and how it had landed him in jail, made it impossible to ignore the desire he felt to have something more, something lasting, with her.

But he knew better. She was still planning to leave at the end of the month.

Van paused and lifted a gloved hand to rub at the center of his chest. He didn't want to feel this way. Yeah, sure, he'd been all in when it became clear they were going to be lovers. And damned if he had any complaints in that department. The woman was open, generous, giving. He grinned. She sure gave.

Lowering his hand, he stared at it. Yesterday, it had taken everything inside of him to hold back from slamming a fist into the face of the man who'd attacked Gabriella. But he'd held back, had kept his temper under control. Part of that was knowing Gabriella would be shocked by his actions.

But the biggest part was that he simply knew he couldn't do it. Oh, he could throw a punch, several of them if needed, but he couldn't pound a man already down, likely beaten, in many ways, before Gabriella had taken him out. It gave him a lift to know that, unlike his father, he didn't have to rely on his fists to feel like a man. To know, without a doubt, that he was nothing like his father.

The only downside to that revelation was that other thoughts, of how this knowledge, this acceptance, might change his view on other aspects of his life, crept in.

Marriage. Family.

Then, she'd planted the seed about him contacting his mother and sister. What he hadn't told her was he knew where they were. Not long after settling in Burton Springs, he'd trolled the internet and found them. He knew his mother still worked at a daycare center and his sister was a social worker. He figured Gabriella would say they'd both used a bad experience to find their way in life.

He couldn't deny Gabriella's suggestion tugged at him, but he still questioned if it wasn't better to leave well enough alone.

Giving up on work, he went to the house and did a few light housekeeping chores. When he heard the sounds of an engine, he walked outside, and his heart kicked against his ribs when he saw her car. What would it be like to do this, feel this, for the rest of his life?

"Hey," she called as she got out of the SUV. "I'm later than I'd planned." She walked over to him, and gripped his shoulders so she could give him a warm, welcoming kiss. "God, it's cold. Christmas is definitely in the air."

"Busy morning?"

"Mostly people stopping by to check on me, pick up any details about yesterday that someone in the gossip chain might have left out."

"What have you got here?" he asked, gaping at the sheer number of the grocery bags she took out of the back seat and passed to him.

"Cookie making supplies. I stopped by Evergreen first. Ellen's letting me borrow the stand mixer and pastry bags." She shot him a glance over her shoulder as she stepped inside the house. "I assumed you didn't have any of that."

"Why would I?"

"Oh, you started a fire."

She set the mixer on the kitchen counter, then walked over to squat in front of the flames. "This is perfect." She held out her hands to warm them. "Or it would be." She rubbed her hands together before standing to slide off her coat. "If there was a nearby Christmas tree."

"I'll get the rest," he said and walked out.

"CHEESE?" HE ASKED. "What kind of cookie has cheese in it?"

"Delicious ones. Italian ricotta cookies." She made a humming noise low in her throat. He'd heard her make something very close to that sound when they made love.

"I like chocolate chip."

"You can have those any time of the year."

Van looked around the kitchen. There were already two kinds of cookies—ones that looked like candy canes, and ones that had been shaped by cookie cutters and frosted—cooling on metal racks she'd brought along. The smells of eggs, butter, and flavorings filled the air. Flour dusted the countertops. Gabriella wore an apron like the one she'd worn the night she'd cooked for him. She'd piled her hair on top of her head but the combined heat from the fireplace and oven had some strands falling loose around her temples.

He wanted this. Not just today. He wanted it forever.

"Gabriella . . ." He stopped when her cell phone rang.

Swiping hands down the front of her apron, she reached for it. "Sorry, I forwarded calls to my cell." Right away, her closed eyes and the trembling hand she used to push at the fallen strands of her hair told him what she was hearing wasn't good. His stomach jittered as he ran through his list of friends, considering all the horrible reasons for that stock-still way she listened.

Once she disconnected, she moved at lightning speed.

"Kids," she explained, stripping off the apron. "Car accident. Last day of school before winter break." She threw on her coat, not bothering to button it, and scooped up her purse before heading for the door. She stopped suddenly, then turned and came back to kiss him hard. "I have to go."

"Let me drive you." He had to hurry to follow her, trying to believe his hammering heart was due to the sprint. "The roads must be a mess."

"I'll be careful," she promised, not looking back. "I'll call when I can."

GABRIELLA PARKED in the middle of the road behind the sheriff's car with its roof lights flashing red and blue. She grabbed her medical bag and ran for the cluster of other vehicles.

"Good thing you were close," Kendall Montgomery told her, leading her to the accident. "The ambulance is on the way, but it's at least a half hour out."

Gabriella knew a half hour could make all the difference in a life.

A single beam from the unbroken headlight speared into the night. Over the odor of spilled gasoline lingered the scent of alcohol. The twisted metal of a crushed front bumper and caved in roof on the overturned car was a horrible contrast to the beauty of the ironwork that Van could create. "Rocking Around the Christmas Tree" blared loud, not quite disguising the car horn. There were moans, cries and the shouts of urgent directions from the officers on scene. She saw one boy, cradling what appeared to be a broken arm as he rocked back and forth, sitting off to the side. The air split with the rip of a saw being jerked to life. Soon the grind of metal on metal drowned out all other sounds as the firefighters worked to crack open the passenger door. The sharp scent of blood had her stomach lurching.

She zeroed in on the passenger seat as soon as they freed space. It took only a glance to admit the girl's chances were slim. Blood bathed her features but Gabriella recognized the girl from the sex education class she'd given at the high school. She'd stayed behind to talk to Gabriella after everyone else had left, asking if her parents would need to be told if she came to the clinic requesting birth control.

Relying on her training and shutting her mind to the fact that this young girl, who'd been smart enough to ask about sexual protection, had obviously been drinking and not wearing a seatbelt, she found a weak pulse. With Kendall's help, she eased the girl to her side, ignoring the moan that movement provoked, to make sure she didn't choke on any blood.

She lost that thin pulse once, but managed to bring it back. Blood coated her hands as she did what she could to staunch the wounds. The temperature hovered in the mid-twenties but sweat rolled down her back and temples.

"Somebody shut off that damned radio," she shouted when "Jingle Bells" merrily rang through the night.

She cursed the lack of equipment, her own training, as she battled for the girl's life. Her hands cramped but they didn't pause. When the ambulance finally arrived, she worked over and around the technicians as they loaded the body and sped to the hospital. During the long ride, she again lost the pulse, but managed to get it started. At the hospital she joined the surgeons, opening that young body, working for hours to repair internal damage, holding onto the thin thread of hope. But in the end, the girl's injuries proved to be too severe.

Shaking off the offer, she went down the hall to the waiting room. Another surgeon had offered to give the devastating news of their daughter's death to the parents, but Gabriella declined. These were people from her town, it was her responsibility to be the one to tell them.

Tired, second-guessing every treatment she'd given that night, she walked away from the tears and grief once the heart-breaking news had been delivered.

She considered calling her mother, asking for reassurance that she'd done everything within her limited ability during the surgery, needing to hear the love and faith that would come through, despite the distance. But for once in her life, it wasn't her mother she wanted to talk with.

"You home?" Van asked when he answered.

"No." She closed her eyes, leaning against the wall.

"You lost them."

"Her." A few tears rolled down her cheeks before she swiped them away. "I couldn't save her. I tried. I tried so hard, Van. I just wasn't good enough."

"You did your best. You gave her a chance."

"If I had more training, maybe I could have done more."

"If you hadn't been here, nobody would have been there to help before they got her to the hospital. Why don't I come get you? You shouldn't be driving when you're so worn out."

She drew in a long breath, opened her eyes. "No. Van, the mayor is here." *Looking as bad as I feel.* "I'll have her drive me back to my car."

"Come back here."

She glanced to her right, zeroed in on the wall clock. "I can't. I have an early appointment. One I can't miss."

"Are you sure?"

She smiled a little. "I'll come by afterward. If that's okay."

"I'll be here."

She disconnected the call, and pushed away from the wall. "Mayor," Gabriella called out.

The woman shook her head. "It's my fault. I'm the one who approved letting the seniors leave early for their Christmas holiday." She looked to the waiting room where she'd left parents numb with pain.

"No," Gabriella said. "They'd been drinking, and they were speeding. It could have happened anytime. They were cele-brating." Sharing the sad bond of regrets and doubts, she wrapped an arm around the older woman's shoulders. "There's nothing else we can do here. Let's go home."

THE NEXT DAY, after a few hours of restless sleep, Gabriella opened the clinic door . . . and smiled for the first time in almost twenty-four hours.

"Come in," she said as Ryland and Sydney Evans approached, hand-in-hand.

"Are you sure?" Sydney asked before she wrapped Gabriella in her embrace. "You must be exhausted."

"I'll sleep later." Maybe, hopefully. She prayed they didn't ask questions or want details. "Besides, I wanted to see you both."

They hung up their coats and hats, and followed Gabriella to her office.

"Is everything okay?" Ryland asked.

"It's all good." Sitting behind her desk, she glanced at Sydney's file before looking at her. "I got the results back from the extra tests I ran."

"The baby?" Sydney said, placing a hand over her stomach.

"What did I just say? There's nothing wrong. Only . . . it's babies, not baby." Gabriella laughed, everything inside of her going soft. "One of the most common reasons for excessive morning sickness is due to multiples. Twins," she clarified when the couple stared at her.

"Two?" Ryland asked.

"We'll know the exact number when we do an ultrasound, but my professional opinion is, yes, you're having two babies."

"Twins." Sydney, her eyes welling up, turned and buried her face against her husband's chest as his arms came around her.

Seeing them, seeing the joy and love between two good people she considered friends, was a joyful boost for a day that seriously needed one.

After Sydney had her cry, Gabriella sat with the couple, going over some specifics, setting up dates for examinations and ultrasounds. While making notations on the files, she tried not to think about not being here to see the babies born.

At the door to the clinic, she reassured the couple, again, that there was nothing to worry about. She also confirmed there was no reason for them to cancel their flight to Boston for

Christmas with Sydney's family. With a laugh, she suggested they get as much rest as they could now.

"You too," Sydney said, leaning over to kiss her cheek. "You look exhausted, Gabriella."

"Then it's good that I have no more appointments today or tomorrow. Drive safe, and if I don't see you beforehand, have a Merry Christmas."

After they left, Gabriella took time to make additional notes in Sydney's file before she locked the door, and left a message on the clinic phone for any incoming calls. Then she dashed upstairs and packed a bag. Before leaving town, she stopped by The Market, using the need to pick up a few groceries as an excuse to check in with the mayor. She was relieved to see the older woman looking more at ease. Then, with the windows rolled down to let the bracing cold sting her cheeks and keep her wits clear, she turned the radio up, and listened to holiday music all the way to Van's place.

As soon as she parked, Van stepped outside of his shop to greet her. Fatigue prevented her from running, but her steps were steady, even as her emotions vibrated and quivered around her heart. Without a word, without question, with the acceptance she only just realized meant the world to her, his arms wrapped around her. With a sigh she lay her head on his chest.

"It was awful," she whispered, her hands rising to stroke along his back. "They were kids, just kids, out of school for Christmas break, filled with joy and wanting to celebrate." As she blew out a breath, it whistled in the cold. She wouldn't tell him of the twisted metal, the odors, the desperation . . .

"You should rest, Gabriella."

He cupped her face, lifting it and touching his lips to hers. "Will you hold me?" she asked. "I know you have work, but will you hold me? For a little while?"

His strong, supportive arms tightened around her. "For as long as you want."

She woke after a two-hour nap. Alone. But he'd held her while she'd drifted off. And when she sat up in his bed, she discovered he'd brought in her overnight bag. Though he'd left her underwear and toiletry bag alone, he'd hung her clothes alongside his in the closet. Humming to herself, she went into the bathroom for a shower, grinned at the *In workshop. Don't cook* note taped to the mirror. Dressed in jeans and a sweater, she tucked the note into a pocket of her overnight bag and headed into the kitchen.

She truly had planned to only make coffee but she loved his kitchen. It was so open and inviting. From where she stood at the counter, slicing carrots for the stew she planned to cook, she could see the big fireplace in the family room. And suddenly, she had an idea. Just because Van didn't want a tree, that didn't mean she couldn't find some evergreen branches and decorate the mantel. Once she had the stew simmering, she got out the mixer and cookie cutters she hadn't yet returned to Ellen. She had the dry ingredients whisked in a bowl when the door opened.

Van scowled. "I told you not to cook."

She shook back her hair, lifting a brow as he removed and hung his coat. He hadn't shaved and his hair was windblown. Her heart skipped a beat. "And you think because we are sleeping together, you can tell me what to do?"

He walked over to her, and took her chin in his fingers. "You still look tired."

"Then . . ." She leaned in and caught his bottom lip between her teeth, feeing the thrill of seeing his eyes darken. "You should have stayed in bed with me." She stepped back and returned her attention to the bowl of ingredients. "Now you've lost your chance."

"It's my kitchen."

"*Si.* And your kitchen is my new love." She slanted him a wicked grin over her shoulder. "Maybe, later, I'll have time for you."

He eyed the messy counter. "This doesn't look like cookie dough."

"*Esatto.* It's for ornaments."

"Even though I don't know what you're saying more than half the time, I love the way your voice sounds when you speak Italian. Wait." He held up a hand. "Ornaments?"

"Dough ornaments."

"I don't have a tree."

"Sad but true. But I thought, if you didn't mind, I'd get some evergreen branches for the mantel. And then we could hang a few of these dough ornaments on it. Although, to be honest, I'm holding out hope you'll cave and get a Christmas tree." She smiled at him as she sprinkled flour on the countertop and began to knead the dough. "Want to help? *Per favore.*"

"You said that on purpose."

Her hands paused a moment in their task. "I need to keep busy, Van. It'll help me more than a nap would."

He studied her, then began to roll up the sleeves of his shirt. "What do you want me to do?"

The ornaments were more misshapen than perfect, even with the help of the cookie cutters, and they would remain salty white rather than colorful, but to her eye, no ornaments had ever been as beautiful or magical. While they cooled, she and Van went outside in search of the best branches to use for the mantel. Of course, they ended up in a silly snowball fight where they both proved to have terrible aim. When Gabriella finally collapsed, stretching out to make a snow angel, she found her body covered and her mouth busy. It was no hardship to dash inside for a shared, steamy shower. With holiday music playing, a glass of wine in hand, and wearing one of Van's flannel shirts, she arranged the branches and hung the ornaments with thin strands of wire he'd unearthed from his workshop.

"It's nice," he admitted when they stood in front of the fire, her hands resting on the arms he wrapped around her waist. "I wish I had a candle." Then he laughed. "Oh hell, I shouldn't have said anything. Because now you'll bring one the next time you come out here."

"You should have two, for balance." She turned, looping her arms around his neck and kissed him. "Two is always better than one."

WHEN SHE WOKE the next morning, Van was holding her close. In the quiet, she realized she had fifteen days left in

Burton Springs, in Van's bed, before she was due to return to Chicago.

With her heart drumming the way it sometimes did when she'd had too much caffeine, she slid out of bed, slipped back into his flannel shirt and went into the kitchen. Standing at the sink, she filled a glass with tap water and stared out the window as the sun began its daily climb above the distant mountains.

Where had the time gone?

She recalled the day she'd arrived in Burton Springs. Those first few days, several people had stopped by, more to check her out than to request medical help. She remembered meeting the people she now considered friends, the times they'd included her in gatherings and activities. And this place—the beauty of wildflowers blooming on the road while snow capped the mountains, the eye-searing blue of the summer big sky—it still made her choke up.

Then, of course, there were the events of the past few weeks. Seeing Van tenderly holding the little girl with the hand wound. The way he looked sitting astride a horse. The gentle way he'd helped Audra and Carter's boys make a paper garland for their tree. The first time they made love . . .

She and Van had created so many memories, way more than she'd ever imagined possible in so short a time.

If she could remember all of those, in such clear and vivid detail, how could she not pinpoint the moment she'd fallen in love with him?

"Dio mio. Dio mio." Her legs gave out and she crumbled to the floor. Arms wrapped around her waist, she pressed her face to her upraised knees. How? When? "What have I done? What have I done?"

What could she do now? She had family and a life in Chicago. Obligations. Goals she'd set long before coming to Montana. And yet, hadn't a part of her enjoyed and flourished doing the kind of medicine she'd done here? Hadn't a part of her been nourished by the knowledge that she could do so much for so many? Look at Mr. James. Even the doctor before her hadn't managed to get him to the clinic for a physical. She'd delivered

Audra's baby. Wanted, with a longing she'd shoved aside to avoid the ache, to deliver Sydney's twins.

"Shh." She jerked a little as Van sat beside her, and cradled her in his arms, sinking his fingers into her hair so he could massage the tension at the back of her neck. Just feeling him, knowing he wanted to soothe what he believed was her distress over a lost patient, had her wondering how she could have ever thought she wouldn't fall in love with him. He was a man with honor and integrity, who hadn't let life make him bitter. How could anyone who knew him, who benefited from his friendship, who'd admired his creativity and talent, not love him, regardless of his past?

There was no one she could talk to about this. With everything else, she'd always gone to her mother. But could she ask her mom, a successful surgeon who'd balanced career with family to be objective when it came to helping her daughter decide whether or not to come home, something Gabriella knew her mother had been looking forward to? And she couldn't talk to her new friends for the same reason. She was sure they'd want her to stay here, just as much as her mother would want her to come home.

How ironic that the one person she could depend on to listen without judgment was the very man currently holding her. The man responsible for all the turmoil in her head and heart.

"You did what you could," he murmured, his lips brushing her forehead with a gentleness that far transcended his strength. "No one blames you for not saving that girl." Another brush of his lips, more gentle strokes of his fingers. "You're just still so tired. I should have made you rest more yesterday."

She shook her head. Whether she did so to silently argue his point or due to the conflict between her heart and her mind, she couldn't have said.

"Today," he said, easing her away so he could lift her face to his. "We'll both take a day off." He kissed her, then smiled. "Would you like to help me pick out a Christmas tree and decorate it?"

"Yes," she answered, resigned to making another memory

with him. Depending on the decision she made, it could be a pleasant one she'd think back on often in the years ahead. Or it could torment her, reminding her of all she'd lost.

So, after a breakfast during which she managed to act as normal as possible, when she swallowed the food her squeezing stomach insisted it couldn't hold down, they dressed and drove to town. At the high school lot, they selected a tree from the dwindling choices, along with two wreaths. Gabriella did her best to ignore the solemn looks of the two young boys who wrapped their selections and helped Van load it all on his truck. With a seductive grin, Van held a branch of mistletoe over their heads.

"Can't forget this," he said as he leaned over to give her a quick kiss. "I'll never again look at a sprig of mistletoe and not think of you."

He looked so carefree and happy that she went along with his mood, doing everything she could to make the most of every moment. Truth was, it wasn't hard. She enjoyed being with him.

They stopped at Unique Finds for candles, along with strings of lights and a few ornaments. Her heart stuttered when she noticed that he'd chosen white lights for his tree. For his home.

Arriving back at his house, after they'd trimmed the tree and danced to Christmas music in the center of his living room, she opened her heart.

Later that night, beneath the mistletoe he'd attached to the headboard, she gave her love freely . . . without saying a word.

Chapter Eight

AFTER TWO uninterrupted days with Van, it felt almost strange to drive back into town, to open the clinic and deal with patients. And yet, it also felt very natural. In addition to asking questions and listening to patient complaints, she took vitals, made notes on charts, ran lab tests. While the work was steady, it didn't feel overwhelming. She admitted to a sense of satisfaction in knowing she covered all aspects of her patient's care.

She hadn't completely dismissed the defeat of losing the girl from the car accident, but the continuity of clinic work helped reestablish her rhythm.

Several hours later, she felt her holiday spirit come to life at the festive atmosphere in town. It reminded her life still held bright spots and reasons to find happiness whenever possible.

"I can't remember the last time I went to a school carnival," she said, her arm looped through Van's. She didn't need to see the looks or hear the whispered comments to understand it was unusual for him to attend community functions. All that mattered was this year, with her, he'd decided to do so.

The halls were decorated with streamers and colored posters made by the students to identify each station, whether it was a game or food booth. Holiday music competed against young children's excited shouts as they pulled their parents' hands toward whatever caught their eye. Teenagers roamed the halls in packs, and the occasional couple. Scents of sugar, coffee, pizza, and popcorn drew people toward the cafeteria.

"Do you want to get something to eat first? Guess not," Van said, answering his own question when Gabriella led him to a booth where the goal was to toss wreaths onto cardboard trees. Promptly ringing three, she accepted a snowflake shaped pencil eraser. Spotting a patient she'd treated last week for an ear infection, she offered the little boy the prize.

"I guess I should be grateful you weren't this accurate with a snowball," Van said, leaning down to brush her lips.

"Now it's your turn to win me something."

"Is that so?"

She loved the sudden twinkle in his eye. She was happy to see him give in to this bit of lighthearted fun, a chance to have a silly childish moment she imagined he'd had so little of in the life he'd told her about.

At the booth set up to resemble ice fishing, he snagged a plastic fish on a magnetic hook and won her a miniature stuffed snowman. They ate slices of pizza that prompted a small pang of homesickness in her, but it was quickly snuffed out when they ran into Ellen and Judson. Then the two couples competed at the penguin race—a narrow trough filled with water, where the contestants blew through straws to move the plastic animals to the finish line.

At the photo booth, Gabriella sat on Van's lap, making funny faces. Then, for the last photo, she turned and kissed him as the camera flashed.

"You play dirty," he complained as they stepped out from behind the curtain to wait on their developed photos.

"Are you just figuring that out?"

"I'll find a way to pay you back."

"Oh." She tossed her hair, then rose on her toes and whispered in his ear, "I'm counting on it."

"Gabriella. Donovan." They turned to see the mayor smiling as she approached them. "It's so nice to see the two of you together. Having fun?"

"Yes. How about yourself?" Gabriella asked.

"Oh, it's hard not to have fun with so much joy in the air." Her smile dimmed a little. "Would you mind, Donovan, if I stole Gabriella away for a bit? I won't keep her long. I promise."

"Why don't I get us some coffee? Would you like some, Mayor?"

"I would." She jerked her head in Gabriella's direction.

"But my doctor keeps telling me I need to cut back on caffeine." She sighed as Van brushed his hand along Gabriella's arm and walked away. "He is a good man."

"Yes, he is. What's going on?" Gabriella asked.

"Why don't we step over here?" She gestured to an empty spot out of the flow of traffic.

"Is something wrong? Someone hurt?" Gabriella sucked in a breath that did nothing to loosen the knot in her stomach. "Is there a legal issue because of the accident?"

"No." She patted Gabriella's arm. "The parents know you did everything humanly possible to save their daughter. What I want to talk to you about is the clinic. You've done a marvelous job. Everyone in town tells me how much they like you, how comfortable they are with you and the way you handle their medical needs. Doctor Leonard was very impressed when I told him you'd managed to get Franklin James in for a check-up."

"Oh, I wasn't aware you'd been in touch with Doctor Leonard. Did he call to tell you when he's returning?"

"He's not."

Gabriella blinked. "Not? You mean at all?"

"Shh," the mayor said, cutting quick glances around. "He said he just can't face coming back to the memories." She met Gabriella's gaze. "The practice is yours, if you want it."

"What?" She took a step in retreat. "But I'm waiting to hear about a surgical fellowship. I should get news any day now."

"Yes, I know. But I'd hoped that maybe you'd reconsider. You've become a part of the community, Gabriella. The entire town would be so much happier having you stay here, instead of trying to find someone new. We need you." When she looked off to the side, Gabriella looked as well . . . and saw Van watching them. "We all need you," the mayor said. "Don't say no right away. Tell me you'll at least think about it."

"Well, God." She tossed up her hands. "How can I not?"

Could she stay? If she did, she could have her own practice, and make some of the changes she believed would benefit the community. She'd be here to oversee Sydney's pregnancy and deliver the twins.

She'd have more time with Van.

But it would mean turning her back on her life-long goal of becoming a surgeon.

"Everything okay?"

Gabriella jumped a little when she realized that while she'd been staring into space thinking, the mayor had walked away and Van had returned.

"Yes, fine. Just some clinic business," she said.

Just my entire life.

GABRIELLA DIDN'T mention her conversation with the mayor to anyone. During her frequent phone calls with her mother, it was hard to keep the questions and possibilities to herself—especially when her mama was so excited about Gabriella returning home in a matter of days. There was no talk of medicine but of planned family gatherings, the returning-home dinner her papa was planning at the restaurant, a mother-daughter day they'd spend getting pedicures and manicures followed by an extravagant lunch.

How could she even consider relocating and leaving her family for good?

But then there was Van. She glanced to her left and felt her heart sigh. He'd made arrangements with Judson to borrow a couple of horses so he could give her a riding lesson. When he added that she'd need to pay attention, she realized he'd noticed her distraction. So far they'd each been quiet. The air was crisp, the sky an eye-searing blue. If her mind wasn't so confused, she'd have enjoyed the moment more.

How could she explain that she'd been offered a chance to change the boundaries of the relationship they'd started? They'd both known going in that their time together was limited. In fact, that was part of the appeal. Just because she'd fallen in love, that didn't mean Van would want to continue if she decided to stay. And how could she ask, without putting him on the spot?

"We should stop."

"What?" Gabriella jerked on the reins. "What do you mean stop?" The horse sidestepped, apparently sensing her distress.

She gripped the reins tighter, using her legs to control the animal the way Van had taught her.

He pointed to a building just visible in the distance. "I know Judson's hoping to purchase that hunting cabin, but for now, it belongs to someone in Georgia, so we should stop and turn around."

"Oh." She rose in the stirrups a little, both to get a better look and to stretch her muscles. "Why does Judson want that cabin?"

"He doesn't so much want the cabin as he wants the land for additional grazing."

Life would go on. Her friends would think of her from time to time, maybe, hopefully. But their lives would go on. Including Van's.

"What about you?" she asked, turning the horse around, waiting for him to do the same. "Ever think about enlarging your workshop?"

"As a matter of fact, I have a meeting at the bank in a couple of days."

"Not with Tammy?"

"She said she would help me, but I thought I'd feel more a part of the town if I went to the bank."

"What are your plans?"

"Enlarge it, like you said. Get some specialized equipment." He paused. "I might add another bedroom to the house."

"That's a great idea," she said, lifting her face to the sky, praying he'd assume it was the sting of the cold air that brought tears to her eyes.

Obviously he had no problem thinking of a future without her.

Once they returned to his house, she decided it would be a good idea to leave. She needed some time alone. But when Van asked her to help him with a special order, she couldn't say no.

So she worked alongside him in his workshop, following instructions, trying not to notice every time their bodies brushed as they wrestled the heated iron to get the detail the way he wanted. It was more than the physical touches, the looks they shared. It was the ease with which they worked together, the way they so often anticipated what the other needed to complete the task.

It reminded her, almost painfully, of surgery—the way nurses would hand instruments to the surgeon, and the choreography of technicians keeping track and announcing changes in vital signs.

And yet there were also silences between them, as if they both sensed the unspoken distress that their days together were coming to an end.

"TELL ME AGAIN how we got talked into this?" Van asked.

"The mayor," Gabriella answered, not meeting his gaze. "She has a way of getting people to do what she wants."

Van watched as she prowled around the workshop. Something was up with her—it had been ever since the accident. But it wasn't the memory of that night that bothered her. Somehow, he knew it was something else. Just as she'd done after the attack, she'd smoothed out her distress after the accident, finding her balance. He wanted to believe he'd helped give her a measure of calm and peace, although, he had to admit, his motivations weren't wholly unselfish.

Not for a minute did he regret the time he'd taken with her. The time they had left was burning away faster than wood thrown into his forge. He'd indulged the fantasy of them as a couple as they picked out a Christmas tree, made the less-than-perfect dough ornaments, decorated the mantel. For the first time since he'd been too young to know better, he'd believed in the magic of the holiday season.

She'd added some other decorations—a music box shaped like a fireplace with a pop-up Santa, a wreath for the door, red plaid placemats to match the single stocking she'd talked him into buying. She'd even managed to sneak in a small train set under the tree.

Unless she had a patient to deal with, she came to his house to spend the night. She cooked, insisting she enjoyed it, that it helped her relax. She still reached for him, accepted him when he reached for her.

But something had changed. *She* had changed. He just couldn't pinpoint how or when.

"Here they come."

Van went to the door to stand beside Gabriella. Rhonda parked the van, then climbed out to open the back sliding door. Four kids, three boys and one girl, stepped onto the porch of the workshop.

"Okay everyone," Rhonda declared. "This is Van Ferguson. And this is his workshop."

"Like Santa and the elves?" the little girl asked.

"Stupid," one boy hissed. "Santa's not real."

Gabriella stepped forward. She didn't reach out to the children—she and Van both had been coached by Rhonda not to do so. Van hadn't needed the warning. Kids who grew up in a violent home learned quickly to avoid being touched whenever possible.

"I'm a doctor," she told all the children. "That means I've studied science for many years. Science depends on facts and research. And yet, I believe, in here." She lifted a hand to her heart. "Santa is the most magical part of Christmas."

"Dr. Santini," Rhonda explained, "is here in case any of you don't follow directions or get nosey and end up hurt." She levelled a glance at all four kids. "I'm sure we won't need her, right?" Four heads nodded in agreement.

"Okay, Van, show us what to do."

"Us?" he asked her, smirking at the way she shivered inside her blanket of a coat.

"I'm not staying out here when it feels like a hot tropical island inside."

Van guided the kids inside, showed them how they would go about shaping iron to resemble a candy cane. Gabriella had brought along red ribbon that they would tie into a bow for each one. He went over safety protocol, reminded them that, because he didn't have additional leather aprons or gloves, he could only work with one kid at a time. The others would have to stand to the side and watch.

Watching them, guiding their eager hands and willing minds, reminded him of his first experiences at blacksmithing. With Rhonda and Gabriella keeping an eye on the kids not working, he handed the last boy, the one who'd stated Santa wasn't real, the gloves. As he tied the string on the apron, the boy put on the gloves and lifted his hands.

"My dad has big hands."

Hadn't he often thought the same thing? Van squatted down, looked the boy in the eye. "So did mine."

Haunted eyes met his gaze. "Did he hit you?"

"Yes," Van answered, hating that the question came so easily to the boy.

"Was it because you were bad?" he asked, his lower lip quivering.

From the corner of his eye, he saw Gabriella look his way, but he kept his focus on the boy. If not for her and her acceptance of his past, her belief in him, he'd never have been able to handle this moment.

"No, it's because he was."

"That's what my mom said."

"Sounds like your mom is pretty smart. For a girl," he added, and was rewarded with the grin he'd hoped to trigger. "You ready to make this candy cane for her?" At the nod, Van rose, settled a tentative hand on the boy's shoulders and walked him through the process.

GABRIELLA RUSHED into Tammy's and the booth where the mayor waited.

"Oh, hell," the mayor said, searching Gabriella's face as she sat. "I had a feeling I wasn't going to like the reason for this meeting." She looked over to the counter. "Tammy, bring me a piece of that pumpkin pie, heavy on the whipped cream." She turned back to Gabriella. "If you're not staying, you have no say in whether or not pie is good for me." She waited until Tammy delivered the slice of pie, buried beneath a mountain of cream, along with a quizzical lift of her brow that neither woman acknowledged. "Go ahead, give it to me straight out," the mayor instructed once they were alone. Gabriella noticed she didn't cut a bite of the pie.

"My grandfather called me this morning." She'd received the call not long after she'd left Van's bed and returned to the clinic. Her parents had called shortly thereafter, their immense pride made all the brighter by their joy of her being home for Christmas. She'd hardly had a chance to say anything. A fact for which she'd been grateful.

"I received notice of my acceptance for the surgical fellowship in my chosen field of pediatrics." Gabriella tore a strip off the paper napkin. "Frankly, I'm pretty sure my grandfather pulled a few strings for me." She tore off another strip. "I keep thinking of that girl I lost in the car accident." She looked up. "I have the chance to learn more and hopefully avoid that kind of failure in the future. Surgery is what I've worked for my entire life."

"I admire that kind of focus and dedication. And I understand how difficult it's been for you to believe, falsely I want to add, that you didn't do enough the other night. But, Gabriella, whenever you think back to your time here, I hope you'll remember all you have done for the people of this town. So many have asked me time and time again what we can do to convince you to stay."

"Leaving isn't going to be easy for me."

The mayor set down her mug, then reached across the table to place her hand over Gabriella's. "It's not going to be easy to let you go. For so many of us." With a light squeeze, she moved her hand back. "When will you go?"

Gabriella swallowed. "In six days."

"Have you told Donovan?"

She shook her head as a single tear clung to her lashes.

TWENTY MINUTES later, rubbing a fist at the ache in her chest, Gabriella returned to the clinic and focused her attention on her few patients. Of course, all she did was delay the inevitable. When the day came to an end, and the clinic closed, there were no more distractions to keep her from facing reality.

With the fellowship, she'd been given an incredible opportunity, one she knew other doctors would envy. She knew her grandfather had opened the door for her, one he fully expected her to not only walk through but shine like the star he believed her to be while doing so.

At any other time in her life, she would have grabbed hold with both hands and met the challenge. It would be hard work, long grueling hours of study. She glanced down at her outstretched hands. What she learned would save lives.

Thinking, she wandered throughout the clinic, stacking magazine selections in the reception area, rearranging brochures of medicine suggestions left behind by pharmaceutical representatives. The clinic could really use a dedicated corner, with toys and books, to entertain the children while they waited.

She approached the horseshoe Christmas tree Van had made. With a shiver, she used a fingertip to trace the edge of the star at the top, a replacement for the one she'd used to stop a robbery. Just as she'd taken action that day, she had to do so now. No one was going to pressure or guilt her into doing something that didn't feel right. Wasn't that why she'd come to Burton Springs in the first place? To take a long, hard look at herself and her goals. Now a big step toward reaching that goal was within reach.

So why did it feel as if taking that step would move her backward rather than forward?

VAN PUT THE final touches on his Christmas gift for Gabriella. He hadn't been sure what he wanted to give her until yesterday. The practicality of her having to pack it for her return to Chicago had prevented a few of his ideas.

Thoughts of not wanting her to leave had nearly stopped him from making her anything. God knew he'd been left behind, figuratively and literally, enough times. Each time, he'd found a way to rebuild his life. To not forget the past, but use it as a lesson and reason to avoid getting hurt again. He'd used it as a wall to keep others from getting too close.

Until Gabriella.

He'd never forget. Not her, not any of the days, or nights, he'd had with her. He'd even begun to wonder if it was possible that he could convince her to stay and build a life with him.

"Foolish," he muttered aloud, his focus broken, something he rarely allowed while working. "She made it clear from the start that this affair was temporary. Be glad you had what you did. Hell." Disgusted with himself, the situation, and the gouge he'd just carved into the copper strands, he tossed aside his gloves and scrubbed his hands over his face.

It wasn't as if he'd be sitting here with his hands stuck in his pockets once she left. For the first time in his life, he felt safe and secure, enough that he was giving thought, in addition to expanding the workshop, to looking for an apprentice. If he did, between the work and the training, he'd be too busy to miss her. To exhausted at night to reach out, wanting to bring her close to him.

"Like hell that'll happen."

He could take a chance, could just come right out and tell her he wanted a future with her. Tell her he loved her. Wouldn't it be better to hear her tell him no? That way, he'd know for sure, even if it hurt every day of the rest of his life. But wouldn't it be better in the long run, instead of always wondering what she might have said, done, if he'd only had the courage to be honest?

An hour later, when a shower had done little to clear his head, he was surprised to hear her car. Granted, there had been days when she'd had few patients so she'd come out and spent the day with him. Sometime he guided her to make simple items in the workshop, other times she kept busy in his kitchen.

But today, she'd mentioned she had appointments most of the day. A sudden, sharp suspicion in his gut kept him motionless. He watched through the wide window in the living room, saw her look to the workshop and wait, as if expecting him. After a moment, she lifted her face to the sky, and drew in a deep breath. God, she looked so lovely, her knees visible between the end of her navy coat and the tops of her boots. She'd wrapped a green scarf around her neck, the same color as the ribbon she'd tied at the tail of her braided hair.

But there was something about the way she stood, about the way she didn't immediately turn and enter the house that told him she had come for a reason other than to spend time together.

Not wanting to hear, he didn't go to her. It was a temporary delay but he'd take every second he could. He turned from the window and started building a fire. He was still watching the flames catch when he heard the door open.

"Van."

His eyes closed at her whispered plea. She hadn't had to give a patient difficult news, but that's what she was about to tell him. Rubbing a hand over one thigh, he rose, turned, and stared at her.

In her eyes, he saw the twin twists of excitement and dread. God knew he'd felt them himself from time to time. But never like what churned in his gut now. He knew enough to be sure he wasn't going to like what she had to say.

She unbuttoned her coat, slipped it off and hung it on the wall peg that she'd adopted as her own. She walked to him, took one hand in hers, squeezed. "I'm sorry, I'm so sorry, but we don't have as much time as I thought, as I'd planned."

"Your family?" he asked.

Her eyes softened as she lifted her hands to frame his face and kissed him. He fisted his hands to stop from reaching for her, from pulling her close. From stopping her from stepping away.

"Of course, you would ask. No, they're fine."

"Something happened."

"Yes." She drew in a breath, and then the words rushed out. "I got the fellowship. The surgical fellowship. It's in pediatrics, which is the field I want. Van . . . ." She held out her hands, looked down at them. "Think about these hands opening tiny little chests, massaging infinitely small hearts, or repairing arteries as thin as fishing line."

She looked up at him, and he saw the stunned delight, the excitement of a challenge glow within her. There was no way on

God's green earth that he could compete with that.

He loved her too much to even consider asking her to exchange her dream for his.

"That's amazing," he said. "You'll be a wonderful surgeon. I'm proud of you, Gabriella."

"It means I have to leave before the end of the year. I have only five nights left."

This he could give her. A smile, a lift of his hand to stroke a fingertip over her cheek. A long, lingering kiss. "Then we'll have to make the best use of the time."

WORD GOT OUT and spread. For the next three days, Gabriella kept busy answering questions, making promises to keep in touch, writing up notes, observations, and reminders in patient files. Packing up the belongings she'd take back to Chicago with her.

Spending her nights with Van.

In the early hours of the morning, when she'd lay in the dawning light pressed against his chest, she had moments where she wished he'd tried to talk her out of leaving. Then, they'd begin their day, sharing coffee and breakfast before separating for work . . . as if they would do so for the rest of their lives. Driving to the clinic, she'd usually admit she'd been foolish to even think that way, before chastising herself for wanting more than was possible. Neither of them had planned on anything more than what they'd enjoyed—a brief holiday affair before she returned to complete her training. Just because she'd fallen in love didn't mean he had.

Because if he had, wouldn't he have said so, especially now when she was poised to leave?

Of course, she hadn't told him she loved him, either, and had had moments when she'd questioned if she truly wanted to leave. Just when she gathered enough courage to raise the issue, he would make a comment about her returning to Chicago, letting her know that he believed she would succeed and become a brilliant surgeon.

How could she protest his obvious willingness to let her go?

"You're quiet tonight," Van said as he drove them out to Evergreen Ranch to have dinner with Ryland and Sydney. She'd been surprised, and a little annoyed, that he'd accepted the invitation without asking her. It wasn't like Van to want to be around other people. And though she knew she was being greedy, she didn't like sharing one of the last two nights they had together with someone else.

"Thinking of what you have left to do before the day after tomorrow?"

Why did he have to know the exact day she'd be leaving? And sound so damned cheerful about watching her walk away? Yes, the fellowship was an opportunity she'd worked her entire life to have. That didn't mean she'd forget him the minute she left.

"I think I have everything taken care of."

His finger tapped on the steering wheel in time to the Christmas carol cheerfully playing on the radio. "Good."

Gabriella closed her eyes and leaned back against the head rest. Even when she realized Van had parked and shut off the engine, she couldn't find the motivation to sit up. But, when his mouth covered hers in a sweet kiss, she found her energy level lifting. She curled a hand over his shoulder, holding him close.

"Umm," she moaned. If she couldn't have anything else of him, she'd take this. For as long as it lasted. "Let's turn around and go home so we can finish this."

He chuckled, then nipped at her bottom lip in the way he had that always stirred her. "Hold that thought."

Her hand closed tighter, stopping his retreat. "I'd rather hold you."

"With an audience?" he asked.

"What?" Finally, she opened her eyes and saw the deep gleam in his eyes that chased away the desire. With a slight nod of his head to the left, she turned her head. "Oh." Her heart melted.

There on the porch of Evergreen's cookhouse, all the friends who'd come to mean so much to her gathered. Beneath a banner that proclaimed *We'll miss you Gabriella.*

"I thought," Van whispered, "that if you had tonight with everyone else, we'd have tomorrow night to ourselves."

She faced him. "This was your idea?"

He nodded. It cracked her heart a little to know that this man, who for so long had held himself apart, had done this for her. She kissed him. "Then let's join the party."

Amid decorations she'd helped hang, she enjoyed wine, music and laughter with good friends.

"I know I'm being selfish, but I really hate that you won't be here to get me through this pregnancy. To deliver our babies," Sydney said, as they stood beside the Christmas tree. Already she'd adopted a pregnant woman's habit of stroking the small mound of her stomach.

"Did I ever tell you I didn't like you at first? I was jealous," Sydney admitted. "It was the day Audra went into labor. You were talking and laughing with Ryland and all I could think about was how, after I left, the two of you would probably get together."

The image was too close to the scenarios Gabriella had imagined about Van with some faceless woman. She gripped the hand Sydney offered. "I know just how you must have felt."

"Then why . . ." Sydney stopped when Gabriella shook her head.

"No, please. Don't."

She kept up the front, revisiting memories, making promises. No one suspected the tug of war that raged inside her.

At the end of the night, as Van drove back to her apartment above the clinic, neither spoke. Silently they climbed the stairs, removed their coats, then turned to one another. And there, where they'd made love for the first time, they again touched, caressed, loved . . . . And the glory that exploded within her, imprinted on her heart.

They slept in each other's arms, waking in the morning to make love again. Over breakfast, they talked of the party, while ignoring the ringing of the telephone downstairs. Today wasn't the time for work—it was for the two of them. Van loaded her packed bags into her SUV before driving his truck to his house.

Before she followed, she took one last walk around the apartment, making sure the lights on the Christmas tree were unplugged, before going downstairs and doing much the same thing in the clinic.

She retrieved the package in her bottom desk drawer and, locking the door behind her, drove to Van's.

He waited for her in the house, where, as was right for this time of the year no matter what time of day, the lights were on the Christmas tree. He'd started a fire and it was there, as they sat knee-to-knee, that she offered the package she'd brought along.

"Hmm," he said, frowning with pretended disappointment. "It doesn't rattle." He lifted and lowered the box in his hands. "Doesn't weight that much, either."

As she laughed aloud, he ripped off the bright paper. Without pause, he lifted the lid on the box, tossing it aside to join the paper.

"Oh, man."

He lifted out the gloves first, followed by the leather apron—all embossed with the new logo of his business.

She'd wanted to give him something to express her respect for his talent and craft, while making sure he remained safe. And a part of her really liked the idea of him wearing something she'd given him, something that would remind him of her.

"This is . . . it's wonderful." He looked up at her, stunned admiration in his eyes. She suddenly realized no one in his adult life, and most likely his childhood, as well, had ever given any thought as to the best gift for him before now. She liked knowing she'd been the first.

"I love it." He swallowed. "Thank you."

Some of the shine dulled a little at hearing him say love without hearing her name. Shaking it off, because even if he had said it, nothing would change, she held out her hand, palm up. "My turn."

With a reverence that tucked itself into her heart, he set the apron and gloves back into the box. Then he ducked far back under the tree and pulled out a small square box.

"Hmm." With her tongue caught between her teeth, she

studied it. "Not nearly as big as my gift to you."

"You don't need an apron. Although I gotta say, I'm really going to miss your cooking."

"I already told you I'd cook tonight."

She ripped the paper much the way he had. And, as he had, she stared, stunned, once the top of the box had been lifted.

Nestled on a bed of cotton was a bracelet made of impossibly thin copper strands braided together, centered by a five-pointed star, an exact replica of the one on the horseshoe Christmas tree he'd made her.

"I read that wearing copper is good for your health. And the star is for what you'll be as a surgeon." He shrugged. "It's my first attempt at jewelry." He paused, then added, "I can't imagine I'll ever have a reason to make more."

How many times could her heart fracture and still continue to beat? "Oh, Van. It's amazing." She lifted it out of the box, and balanced it on her palm. "Will you slide it on for me?"

It was so light, she hardly noticed it on her wrist. Of course, she'd always know it was there, would always know it had been made special for her, then placed there by the man she loved.

The words trembled on her lips, at the tip of her tongue. But she bit them back before they could spill out. He'd given her no reason to believe he expected more than a night of memories and sex before they said good-bye. She wouldn't mar their last night with declarations that might be met by silence.

She adopted his casual attitude as they went outside and played in the snow, then came back inside and warmed each other by the fire. With just the two of them, she'd decided to forego the Italian traditional seven fishes menu for Christmas dinner and instead prepared handmade lasagna.

Throughout the rest of the day and night, she refused to acknowledge the ticking clock in her head. They talked and touched without pause, as if by doing so they could delay the inevitable. It wasn't until the early morning, as she lay nestled in Van's arms, her body warm from their loving, that she faced the reality that their time together had run out. Sure, she could stay in his bed until daylight. But nothing would change.

Slowly, refusing to look back, she climbed out of bed. She continued to avoid looking at Van as she dressed. She knew he was awake. She prayed as she never had before that she could escape before he said anything.

Still, with her hand on the doorknob, she paused. He wouldn't understand the words, but remembering how he'd once said he loved her voice when she spoke Italian, she hoped he heard the love she couldn't acknowledge.

"Ti amo," she whispered and went outside to her car.

Chapter Nine

SHE DIDN'T CRY. Her eyes might have burned, but she attributed that to focusing on the road lit only by her headlights after so little sleep. She didn't relive memories, didn't consider regrets, didn't second-guess decisions.

She would have continued blindly driving if not for the first peek of the sun over the horizon shooting her in the eye as it reflected off a fender.

The truck was parked on the shoulder, exhaust from the running engine puffing into the cold air. Gabriella saw the shadow of one head rise up, then what looked like an arm wave before it disappeared. Frowning, she glanced in her rearview mirror, then tapped the brakes to slow as she passed the truck. She hesitated an instant longer, but her instincts were humming, so she pulled to the side and stopped.

Cautious, she approached the truck, a large one with a back seat compartment. "Hello," she called out, knocking on the rear door. It popped open, startling her into stepping back. A pungent odor poured out with the heat of the interior.

"Help," said a young man, probably not much more than twenty. "It's my wife. She's in labor."

Gabriella climbed into the truck cab. There was some scrambling to make room in the crowded back seat, with the man kneeling on the floorboard.

"I'm a doctor." She saw the woman, a girl really, her shoulders pressed against the door. Her breathing sounded loud and labored within the truck interior. Her dark hair was matted, and her eyes showed every fear running through her. Her hands cradled her distended stomach.

The young man laid one of his hands, large and rough enough to remind her of Van's, over his wife's as his other hand gently stroked her hair. But it was the woman's hand that captured her attention. The nails had a faint blue cast to them. Gabriella looked up, made an immediate diagnosis and began calculating procedure.

"I'm Gabriella Santini."

"Jesse Simmons, ma'am. This is my wife, Angela."

"How far along are you, Angela?"

"Thirty weeks," she managed to say between breaths. "I—" She sucked in a breath, tears gathering in her eyes as she looked at her husband. "I have asthma. Is our baby going to be okay?"

"This is the season of miracles. I'm going to do everything I can to make sure that record continues." She looked at Jesse. "Did you call the hospital?"

He nodded. "Before we left the house. Then, when Angela started having trouble breathing, I called again. They said by time an ambulance could get here, we could already be at the hospital, and that would be better for her and the baby."

"I asked Jesse to stop." Angela paused, breathed through a contraction. "My water broke." She looked up at him. "I needed him."

"Right now, I need him to go back to my SUV," Gabriella said, keeping a close eye on Angela as she gave instructions. "There are two medical black bags in the back compartment. Bring them both. There should also be a blanket." She tried to remember what she kept on hand during her months in Burton Springs. "And a couple of towels, and some bottled water. Bring all of it."

She felt tears burn her eyes when she saw the tender way Jesse leaned down to kiss Angela and murmur some whispered promise. Then, with a pleading look for her, he wedged around her and out of the truck. She figured he'd make a speed record in his trip to retrieve her bags.

"I should examine you. Can you lift your hips a little?"

Angela nodded and together, she and Gabriella managed to slide her damp jeans off. As much to relax the young woman as to gather information, Gabriella asked, "Do you know if you're having a girl or a boy?"

"No, we wanted to be surprised." Her laugh caught on a quick, indrawn breath. "Boy, we're getting our wish."

The door opened and Jesse returned, juggling his load. He handed it off to Gabriella, then rushed back to his wife's side.

"I'm fine," Angela reassured him. She smiled. "Better than you'd be if we switched places." Jesse paled. "Look at that, Doctor. The big strong cattleman can't stomach the thought of pain."

"I know someone like that, a blacksmith. He's another strong man who practically faints at the mention of a needle."

"Is he the one who made your bracelet?" Angela asked.

"Yes, as a matter of fact, he did."

"It's beautiful."

"It's the only piece of jewelry he's made."

"Then he must think you're very special."

Gabriella looked down, her heart drumming as she studied the bracelet, thought of the hours of work involved in the design and crafting of the metal. He was the special one, a man who'd risen above his past. A man unlike any she'd ever known.

"Doctor?" Angela asked, her voice strained.

"He really is talented, isn't he?" she asked, shaking off her personal thoughts. She needed to focus on her patient, give Angela the best possible care under less-than-ideal circumstances.

She completed her cursory exam, determined they were close enough to delivery that they were better off staying where they were. She took vitals, and made a record of them on her tablet. As Jesse coached Angela through another contraction, she noted down the time.

"Do you own your own ranch, Jesse?"

"No, ma'am. I'm hired on at Shadow Mountain Ranch."

"That's how we met," Angela said. "My daddy is Raymond Quinn's attorney and I was delivering some paperwork out at the ranch. I saw Jesse while I was walking around waiting for Mr. Quinn to finish up reading and signing the papers. We started talking."

"As soon as I saw her, I knew I'd never want anyone else."

She sighed, and her cheeks turned a pretty shade of pink. "I got the papers from Mr. Quinn, but I didn't make it back to town until the next morning."

"I thought her daddy was going to come after me with a shotgun." His grin faded. "He probably should have. Angela was less than a month away from leaving for law school."

"I was only going to please my daddy," she interrupted. Her hand lifted to cup his cheek. "I found something I wanted more." She looked back at Gabriella. "I had to be the one who proposed."

"I wasn't going to be the one who stopped you from going to school."

"I didn't want to go," she said, spacing each word with intention—and effort—as she struggled to catch her breath. "I wanted to be with you." She grew silent, drawing in shallow breaths.

"We could have waited until you got through with school," Jesse said.

"Someone else will have to be the lawyer. I didn't want to wait. I wanted you."

"I don't want you to ever regret the choice you made, Angela."

"How could I when you, and our family, are all I want."

Tears in her eyes, Gabriella watched the couple lean into one another, pressing their foreheads together. They were so young and yet so sure they could handle whatever came their way.

Just as they handled the next hour while the contractions built in frequency and intensity. Twice, she did all she could to get Angela through her asthma attacks. Twice, she worried about the potential consequences for both mother and child. And twice, she mentally acknowledged that if she hadn't stopped, the child, and possibly the mother, wouldn't have survived on their own.

It wasn't easy. There wasn't much room. For the most part, everyone laughed about the close quarters and forced intimacy. Gabriella had handled several births during her years as an intern and resident, although not in the cab of a truck parked on the side of the road. Still, she'd never before seen a couple so in sync with one another. When Angela's energy flagged, Jesse found ways to encourage her, to lift her spirits. When he got shaky with nerves, and once when it looked like he might pass out, she teased him to calmness.

"You're doing great," Gabriella said, hours later, rubbing more hand sanitizer onto her hands. Lifting the blanket, she took a look. "I see a whole lot of dark hair," she said, smiling at the squeak coming from Jesse. "Why don't you try and squeeze in behind Angela to support her." She couldn't help teasing. "Unless you want to come down here and have a front row seat."

"Uh, no thanks." He scooted behind Angela, their hands linking tight over her belly. "I've helped birthed my share of cows, but I'd just as soon you do the honors here, Doctor."

She really had to do little more than encourage before watching the miracle of life come into her waiting hands. Angela collapsed against Jesse's chest. "There's no crying," she said, despite her obvious exhaustion, as well as struggling for her own breath.

"Don't worry." Gabriella gently stroked a fingertip down the slope of the child's nose, then lowered it to thump it against the bottom of a tiny foot. "Told you," she said, with a huge grin, and not a little relief, when the baby let out his first cry. "Congratulations, Mom and Dad, you've got a healthy son. Lift your shirt a little higher, Angela. Putting him on your bare chest will be good for both of you."

While the new parents took in the sight of their son— neither was shy about shedding happy tears—Gabriella took care of tending to Angela. She could, at least privately, admit to being relieved that the birth had gone as well as it had. She'd be even more relieved once they reached the hospital and the doctors could have a look at mother and son.

The sun had risen, had stood high in the sky, and was now heading for the horizon. Between her emotional night with Van, along with the stress and excitement of this day, her body was heavy with fatigue. She wrapped the baby in a receiving blanket taken from the bag the couple had brought with them and then helped Angela guide that tiny mouth to her breast.

"I really hate to break up this moment," Gabriella said, watching closely as the baby ignored the offering. Angela continued to patiently rub the nipple over his mouth. "But, Jesse, it's going to be best for everyone if you can get us to the hospital. There's no need to rush, no reason to get there fast, but the sooner we can get your wife and son in more comfortable surroundings, the better."

"You'll ride with us?" Angela asked.

"Yes."

So she left her vehicle behind and sat with mother and baby, monitoring each of them, as well as recording as many details as she could on her tablet, while Jesse drove them the two hours to the hospital. She stayed with them through admission, through the explanation of facts and details of the delivery to the attending physician. At Angela and Jesse's request, she stayed through the examinations of both mother and son. By time the baby had been settled in the NICU for overnight observation and the parents were in a room, it was well past midnight. Having done so more times than she could count, Gabriella collapsed onto a skinny bed in the doctors' on-call room, and let exhaustion keep doubts, questions, and longings at bay.

When she woke after six hours of dead sleep, she grabbed a cup of coffee and immediately headed for the NICU. The story of her doing the roadside delivery had circulated throughout the hospital and nurses gave her a gown and mask before allowing her entry into the nursery. Six incubators held infants—all wearing red Santa caps. When she spotted the correct incubator, her heart skittered in her chest.

"Angela and I agreed." She turned to see Jesse, standing behind the wheelchair where his wife smiled at her. "It was only right to name him Gabriel."

Angela reached for her hand, squeezed tight. Gabriella swallowed down an emotion she couldn't identify. "Thank you for stopping to help. Thank you for everything you did to get us through those long hours, to give us our son. Thank you."

She spent an hour of indulging herself with the new family, and then took time to speak with the newly arrived grandparents. Intending to call for a ride, she said her goodbyes, but was stopped from leaving when Jesse insisted on driving her back to her SUV. Once he'd parked behind her vehicle, he spoke.

"I can't begin to thank you enough, Doctor." He faced her with unashamed tears in his eyes. "If you hadn't stopped and helped us, I could have lost them both."

"They would have been fine," she hastened to reassure him. "Nature usually manages without human interference."

"No." He shook his head, took off his cowboy hat, stared through the windshield. "We were out here in the middle of nowhere. I told you the hospital said they couldn't get to us any quicker than we could drive there." He looked at her. "If not for you, I don't know, don't want to think about, what might have happened."

"Nothing did. Next time, add in some extra travel time." She reached over and patted his arm. "You go on back now and be with your wife and son. It's your turn to take care of them."

"Yes, ma'am. I'm going to make them proud."

"I believe you will."

She sat in her vehicle, letting the engine warm, and watched in the rearview mirror as Jesse turned his truck around and headed back to the hospital. While she'd dismissed his praise about what she'd done, she ran events through her mind, reviewed procedures and realized how lucky they had all been. She'd saved that baby boy's life. And possibly his mother's, too.

She had been in the right place at the right time to help. Maybe it was fate or just luck that had caused their paths to cross. The reality was, this family had had no one else but her to depend on. She shifted, staring out the window at the wide expanse of snow-covered fields.

She hadn't needed surgical skills, just the basic training she'd called upon so often during this past year. While in Burton Springs, she'd learned that compassion and patience were as essential as her knowledge. Tending to the everyday things, the small miracles along with the occasional emergency, was every bit as important, as essential, as the urgent or life-threatening cases.

Had she been so blinded by the long view, been so seduced by the prospect of surgery, that she'd neglected to see what fulfilled her soul as much as her professional goals?

She wanted to call Van, to talk to him, tell him the thoughts and questions running like thunder through her mind. She wanted to tell him about her terror of failing that young family, her joy at succeeding. The stunning pleasure of having a newborn slip into her hands, of giving him into the love and care of his parents.

She could picture his face as he listened to her, as he brushed aside her confession about those seconds of panic with his confidence in her. No one—not her parents, her grandfather, or any of her colleagues—had ever had the kind of faith in her that Van did.

Tears blurred her view.

That was the reason he hadn't stopped her from leaving. Not because he believed he wasn't good enough for her. Not because he didn't love her. He did. He'd shown that love, that faith, by letting her follow her dream.

Her finger rubbed the copper braid on her wrist.

Dreams could change. Hers had changed. And this new dream would make her life fuller, richer. If she was brave enough to reach for it. There was so much she could do, wanted to do. There would be no regrets, no thoughts of missed opportunities. No guilt for making the choice that was perfect for her. Just as not everyone could, or should, be a surgeon, not every doctor could, or should, have the widespread knowledge necessary to tend so many different people and situations.

It was more than practicing medicine, it was being part of a community. Sharing the joys and heartaches of friends. Building a life with the man she loved.

What better day to realize, to plan for that new dream, than on Christmas Eve?

She reached for her phone, then punched a button on her speed-dial. "Mama," she said, smiling. "I need your help."

FOR THE FIRST time in his life, Van wished he had a bottle of whiskey. Instead, he stood in the center of town—where he damn well had not planned to be—his shoulders hunched against the wind and light snow . . . and against the sympathetic looks he'd been getting since the mayor had all but bullied him into being at the gathering in front of the big tree for the Christmas Eve celebration.

Only he didn't feel like celebrating. Everyone in town knew he'd been seeing Gabriella. And everyone in town knew she'd left. Why couldn't they just leave him alone?

Life had been so much easier when he'd kept to himself. When he hadn't opened himself up to this kind of ache.

Only he had. With Gabriella. With her he'd felt more, had started to believe in a life he'd never before considered. Hell, he'd even put up a Christmas tree. Nothing meant anything without her. What did he care about peace on earth or joy to the world when his life had been shattered?

His past be damned. He deserved happiness as much as the next person. Gabriella had given him that gift. Maybe some people would look at him different, treat him different, if they learned about the things he'd done. He knew with others it would make no difference. It hadn't mattered to Gabriella, and her opinion was the only one that meant anything to him. With her by his side, he could face whatever came.

He had more possessions than he'd ever had, but he didn't have the one thing—the one person—he needed to make his life complete. He'd remade his life before. He could do it again. He'd wash dishes in her father's restaurant, if need be.

He just had to find a way to be by her side.

"You don't look like you're in the Christmas spirit," the mayor said, tipping the flame of her candle to light his. He decided the best thing to do was to remain as silent as the night that the choir would soon be singing about.

"As for myself," she continued, nodding her head at Rhonda and Sheriff Owens as they walked by, "I had a marvelous day, one filled with a wonderful surprise." She chuckled. "After all, it wouldn't be Christmas Eve without a Christmas miracle."

"What does this have to do with you wanting me to be here tonight?"

"You disappoint me, Donovan. I thought a man as tough and determined as you are, one who's turned his life around and become someone I'm happy to know, a businessman I'm proud to have associated with our town, would have more courage. Of course, I know," she added, when he couldn't find the words to ask. "I check out everyone who comes to this town, wanting to become a part of it. What I learned only made me respect you more. I'm not the only one."

As the choir began singing, she smiled, then slipped his candle free, and stepped to the side.

Van blinked.

She looked like an angel walking his way. Whether it was illusion or in anticipation of overhearing their conversation, the crowd quieted. The candlelight surrounding them made the tears in her eyes seem to twinkle. His gaze never left Gabriella's.

He wanted to go to her, meet her halfway. Touch her. Gather her close. Prove she wasn't his imagination. Only his feet wouldn't move.

Her lips trembled with a small smile. She looked tired and yet she'd never before looked more beautiful.

"You let me go," she whispered when she reached him.

"I couldn't stop you from going after your dream."

Her smile grew, as if enjoying a secret, puzzling him. "What if I want a different dream?"

He started to shake his head, to deny her claim. Only he wanted to believe. He wanted, he realized with a small smile of his own, to believe in a Christmas miracle.

"What kind of dream do you want now?" he asked.

"To do good work, the kind of work others depend on. To be where people need me." She took a small step forward. "I dream of having friends, being part of a community that cares and takes care of its own." This time he took a step forward, bringing them nearly toe-to-toe. "I dream of being with the man I love." She drew in a breath, held it, let it out. Her gaze stayed on his, even as he spotted the nerves, so like the ones jumping in his stomach. "And, hopefully, someday have a family with him."

"I never dreamed when I was a kid," he said, not caring who overheard. "Didn't see any point in it when most days were lousy and the same as the ones before."

He glanced over, gave the mayor, along with Rhonda standing beside her, a small nod. Then he realized the sheriff, along with Kendall Montgomery, were keeping people back, giving them space. He looked back at Gabriella, and reached for her hands. Once again, they were cold because she hadn't taken time to put on her gloves. He could warm them, would always want to warm them for her. And give her anything else she needed.

"I promised myself that I would never depend on anyone else, in any way, for any reason."

"What happened?" she whispered when he grew silent.

"I'll always regret the way it came about, but I discovered work that I enjoy, work I'm good at. I found, after a few missteps, my place, somewhere I have friends that I can depend on, if need be." He lifted her hands, kissed her knuckles. "I found a woman who accepted me without question. A woman I could dream of spending the rest of my life with." His hands squeezed hard. "I have big hands."

"I know," she said with a delighted purr that shot straight to his groin.

"I'll never use them on you."

"Oh, Van. I know."

"Or the children I want to have with you." A tear rolled down her cheek. "Gabriella, you're the only one I've ever wanted to have a family with. You're the woman I love, that I want to love for the rest of my life."

He drew her toward him and wrapped her in his arms. "Tell me," he said. "Tell me you love me in Italian."

"*Tio amo.*"

He smiled. Her tears streamed down her cheeks, flavoring their kiss. Cheers erupted around them. "I was coming for you," he said, breathing hard. "I would never stop you from going after your dream, but I was coming for you. I would have found a way for us to be together. I never considered that you would come back." His heart raced against hers. "So be sure, Gabriella, be very sure, that staying here is what you want."

She lifted the hand where his bracelet circled her wrist. "I don't need to be a star. I need you. I love you, Van. You and the life we can have together are what I want."

"Then you have seven days."

"What?"

"I want to start the new year with you as my wife." Her eyes went wide and she made a choked sound in her throat. "We'll go home," he said when she opened her mouth. "We'll call your family. Somehow, I'll find a way to get them here. Marry me on New Year's Eve, Gabriella. Start a life with me."

"You want me to plan a wedding in less than seven days."

"Yes."

She glanced around them, surrounded by the friends and community they both loved. Lights from the Christmas tree, and the candles still being held by the crowd, added warmth to the cold night air. At a gesture from the mayor, children began to sing as they rang the small bells in their hands. Gabriella faced him with a smile as bright as any star in the night sky. It certainly brought a glow to his heart.

"*Sí*."

Epilogue

GABRIELLA STARED at her reflection. What a difference a week made. She smiled.

Seven days ago, she'd been heartbroken as she drove away from the man she loved. Today she would stand beside him and make promises for a lifetime. In between, she'd helped bring the miracle of new life into the world. And the wonder of friends and family pulling every string imaginable, doing every task needed, to ensure that the small ceremony due to begin in less than an hour went off without a hitch.

Flowers had been brought in to transform Evergreen's cookhouse into a romantic setting for both the wedding and reception. Rhonda had helped her shop for her dress and shoes—her smile tilted at a wicked angle—along with some very nice lingerie. The mayor had expedited as many of the details of Gabriella buying the clinic as she could. Audra and Ellen made all the food for tonight—except for what her papa had insisted on cooking.

And because Sydney and Ryland had decided to cut short their family holiday visit to be here for the wedding, her entire family had been able to fly to Montana on the Bishop Foundation's private jet.

The one thing family and friends had not done, after Christmas Day, was allow Van and Gabriella to spend the night together. Still, they'd managed to sneak in a few intimate moments in the most interesting places.

"*Avanti,*" she called out at the knock on the door. Only it wasn't her parents as she expected.

"Oh, don't you look wonderful," Van's sister exclaimed as she shut the door behind her.

This was another thing that had been accomplished in the short week. Asking her to sit beside him, Van had called his mother and sister. Through tears and apologies, the fractured family took the first step toward reconciliation and forgiveness. Two days ago, Van's mother and sister had arrived in Burton Springs, along with his sister's husband and two-month-old son. There had been more long talks, a few bumps, but the bond had held steady.

"I hope you don't mind," Rosie said. "I wanted to give Mom and Donovan some time alone."

"Of course not." Gabriella held out her hands. "He's so happy you came."

"He's happy." Rosie's hands squeezed. "You make him happy."

"Don't you make me cry."

"Happy tears, Gabriella." She bit down on her bottom lip, a gesture Gabriella had already learned meant she was intent about what she was about to say. She took a tissue from the pocket of her dress and dabbed under Gabriella's eyes. "I can't thank you enough for helping Van contact us. For loving him."

Rosie stepped back, and smiled. "I love being a mom." Her eyes, green like Van's, twinkled. "I'm going to love being an aunt."

Gabriella laughed. "And I'm going to love having you as a sister."

Alone again, Gabriella pressed a hand to her stomach. The nerves that jumped were anticipation and eagerness. She'd changed the direction of her life—personal and professional. And she couldn't be happier.

She turned when the door opened.

"Oh, baby."

"Don't you dare cry," she instructed as both her parents walked in.

"How can I not?" Noelle Santini, elegant in a simple dress of dark green, walked to her only daughter. "You glow." Her hands lightly settled on Gabriella's shoulders as she kissed both cheeks. "He makes you happy."

"I love him so much, Mama."

"It shows."

"It means so much, to both of us, that you and Papa like him." Not only liked, but accepted, when Van insisted on telling them everything about his past. She held out a hand to her father, who looked handsome in his dark suit and tie that matched his wife's dress.

"He's a good man," he said, his eyes misting. "Even though he'll be keeping my baby so far away."

"I did what I had to do. What I needed to do."

"We know that." Her mother shared a look with her father and she knew they'd talked, probably cried together over the knowledge of the distance that would separate them. And yet, they accepted her choice. It was no less than they'd done at every other time in her life. Even her grandfather, although disappointed, had not seemed surprised by her decision to give up the surgical fellowship. There would be tough days ahead she knew, when she'd miss her family like a limb. But she had complete faith that the man she loved, the one she would soon walk toward, would ease that ache.

The three of them shifted toward the knock on the door. Kathy Davis stuck her head inside. "We're ready for you, Mrs. Santini."

After one last hug, her mother left the room. Then, giving her papa a heartfelt hug, she allowed him to escort her out of the room.

She wasn't nervous. Anxious, yes, she was ready, more than, to begin her life with Van. "Papa," Gabriella said, stopping them before stepping into the big room. She leaned over and kissed his cheek. "You'll always be my first love."

Then she took the step that would give her love, forever, to another man.

Van kept his gaze locked on hers as she walked to him. For her, there was no one else in the room. Then, as she came to a stop, her lips curved as she followed his pointing and looked up.

"I told you," he said. "I'd always think of you whenever I see mistletoe."

So, surrounded by family and friends, beneath the delicate iron ball of interlocking mistletoe leaves and hearts custom made by the groom, they exchanged their vows.

And sealed those life-long promises with their first kiss as husband and wife.

The End

Author Biography

An author of passionate, emotional romances with heart, Pam loves crafting stories about independent women and men who discover the thrill and joy of falling in love. After years of moving as both an Army brat and corporate wife, Pam and her craftsman husband settled in Atlanta, close to family and friends. When not writing, Pam enjoys quilting, planting beautiful flowers, home improvement projects and spending time with her wonderful family.

Connect with Pam at:

pammantovani.com

Newsletter Sign-up: eepurl.com/TopgX

twitter.com/mantovanipam

facebook.com/Pam-Mantovani-347988868649487/

pammantovaniauthor@gmail.com

instagram.com/pammantovaniauthor/

amzn.to/2Euk85J

goodreads.com/author/show/3041797.Pam_Mantovani

bookbub.com/profile/pam-mantovani

allauthor.com/author/pammantovani/